# SECRETS TO DIE FOR

### A DI KAREN HEATH CRIME NOVEL

### JAY NADAL

Published by 282publishing.com

Copyright @ Jay Nadal 2023

All rights reserved.

Jay Nadal has asserted his right to be identified as the author of this work.

No part of this book may be reproduced, stored in any retrieval system, or transmitted in any form or by any means, electronic, mechanical, photocopying, recording or otherwise, without the prior written permission of the author.

This book is a work of fiction, names, characters, businesses, organizations, places and events other than those clearly in the public domain, are either the product of the author's imagination or used fictitiously. Any resemblance to actual persons, living or dead, events or locales is entirely coincidental.

# 1

*ONE WEEK AGO. Manchester.*

Whimpers filled the deserted warehouse, a cavernous space with broken windows offering an open invitation for the wind to howl through. Echoes of loneliness whispered through the shattered glass. Old newspapers swirled round on the floor, their rustling providing a distraction for the man tied to a chair, his head bowed, blood dripping from a split lip and a broken nose.

Encircling him stood four burly men with menacing, cold eyes filled with hatred and anger.

"This isn't going your way, is it?" Harman suggested as he stepped through his four associates and took his place in front of Vincent "Vinny" Silver. He leaned in and grabbed Silver's hair, yanking the man's head up so he could stare him in the eye. "Look at me when I talk to you!" Harman yelled, his words booming through the unit.

Silver opened one of his swollen eyes.

"That's better. Now where is he?" Harman asked.

Panic clawed at Silver's chest. "I swear I don't know. I've looked. Honest. I… I."

Silver didn't have time to finish as Harman launched a thundering right jab, which landed squarely on Silver's nose. Silver screamed as blood splatters flew in every direction.

Harman tutted as he wiped the blood from his hands. "I gave you a grand to find him and then you disappeared. Think you can run off with my money?" Harman yelled as he stepped back and nodded at one of his associates.

A stocky, bald man stepped forward and launched a volley of body shots with fists the size of a club hammer head. Silver squealed like a pig as he doubled up, desperate to protect himself from the worst.

Silver's body weakened and his mind shattered as he folded further into the chair.

Harman stepped in again. "You gave it the big one, didn't you? You told me you had all the connections to find him and my money. But you lied. You took my grand and went underground for three weeks. I've been looking for over a year now and you promised an end to my search." Harman gritted his teeth as his temper raged. "You said you had the contacts, and you knew the right people. It was nothing more than lies. I had to send people to find you. Do you know how much of a waste of time it was for me? No, I guess you don't."

Silver looked up, his eyes meeting Harman's. "Believe me. I honestly don't know where he is. I tried; I did. But no one has seen him, and we couldn't find him in the system."

Harman let out a deep sigh. "Excuses. Excuses. Do you know how sick I am of hearing you whine and moan?"

Harman moved to one side as one of his associates came round behind Silver and wrapped his thick arm round Silver's neck and tightened his grip. Silver coughed and spluttered as his eyes grew wide. He gasped for breath as tears squeezed from the corners of his eyes. A jumble of words tumbled from his lips. Harman gave his man the nod, the associate loosening his grip and stepping back.

"You see, we could play this game with you all day long. But we have better things to do. We could kill you right now. Chop you up in a dozen pieces and bury you under a ton of concrete at the nearest construction site." Harman laughed. "But where's the fun in that? I need you to get a message out for me. We're going to let you go, and I want you to go out there and tell everybody I'm looking for him. Understand?" Harman leaned in and studied Silver's face.

Silver nodded, his face bloodied and bruised, his eyes dancing round in their sockets as he struggled to focus.

"I didn't want to do this, but you've left me no choice. I hate calling in favours, but sometimes jobs like this need a specialist and there's only one man for it." Harman glanced over his shoulder and beyond the circle of his associates to a dark figure lurking in the shadows, his leather jacket catching the light as he took a few steps forward, each footstep slow and measured. The associates backed up to allow him through.

The tall muscular figure of Cready appeared, and with him came an ominous shadow that announced his presence long before words were spoken. His black bald head glistened under the fluorescent lighting. Dressed all in black, like the messenger from the dark side, it felt as if the air chilled round him as he stood in front of Silver. He glanced at the victim and studied him for a few moments before looking across to Harman, who gave him a nod.

It was a cue for Harman's associates to grab Silver and hold him in place as Cready stepped forward.

Silver looked up; his eyes wide in fear as the dark stranger loomed over him. Rapid gasps tore from his throat as he squirmed in the chair. The harder he resisted, the more the associates held him in place.

"Please. Please. I promise I'll find out everything you need to know. Don't hurt me any more," Silver cried, "I can't. I can't."

Cready reached into the inside pocket of his jacket and pulled out a pair of tin snips.

Silver cried and screamed as he thrashed in his chair, the associates bearing weight down to hold him in place. One associate reached out and grabbed Silver's right hand, pressing his fingers flat against the armrest of the chair.

Cready stepped in and grabbed Silver's little finger, separating it from the rest of his hand before wrapping the blades of the tin snips round the base and squeezing.

Silver's ear-piercing screams tore through the building as the blades crunched through the digit with the unmistakable crack of a bone before the little finger fell to the floor. He sobbed uncontrollably as he raised his head to the ceiling, his cries turning into a high-pitched wail as waves of pain flooded his body.

Cready wiped down the blades of his tin snips before replacing them in his pocket and stepping back.

Impressed with what he had seen, Harman nodded his approval. "The job is yours. Find him. The price on the street is five grand for information on where he is, plus your fee. If anyone gets in your way, get rid of them."

Cready nodded in Harman's direction before walking away.

Harman bent down to inspect the bleeding stub on Silver's right hand, sucking in air through his teeth. "Whoa. Looks nasty. You'll live. Let it be a warning to you and everyone else. No one crosses me. You've seen a taste of what Cready can do. There's a reason he's called the Silent Assassin. He doesn't say much, but he gets the job done." Harman turned and walked away, heading towards the nearest exit. "Cut him loose and dump him on the street, boys."

# 2

*Present-day. York.*

"Stop, you silly woman!" David shouted at his wife Mary.

She'd been diagnosed with dementia a few years ago, and recently, he'd noticed a sharp decline in her cognitive ability. Simple tasks like putting on a pair of socks were now a challenge for her; so much so, that he'd reluctantly paid for private healthcare assistants to visit several times a day to help her.

A concerning development he'd noticed was Mary randomly calling out other names like Patrick or Stephen, but he didn't know anyone by those names, and so put it down to her illness.

"How many times have I got to tell you? It doesn't go on your hand!" He glared at her and tutted. Tired and exhausted with this daily ritual, his frustration boiled to the surface.

Mary Cooper sat on the edge of the bed with her fluffy sock on her right foot, the left sock on her left hand. She looked across at her husband. Her look had an air of innocence about it, as if she didn't know what to do next.

David walked over to the bed and pulled the sock off. He dangled it in front of her face for her to see. "This is a sock." He pointed at it. "It goes on your foot," he added, gesturing towards her bare foot. "It does not go on your bloody hand."

"I was only doing my hair, David. There's no need to shout at me."

"You don't comb your hair with a bloody sock," he groaned, tossing the sock on to the bed and taking a few steps back towards the window. He turned and stared at the garden as he pressed his palms into the windowsill. Frustration and sadness gnawed away at him. It was a full-time job just to care for his wife and not something he could do for the odd hour here and there. It was a twenty-four-seven commitment, and one he was struggling with at his age. His body grew tired, his mind became frazzled, and with each passing week, he found it more difficult to remember everything, such as her medication schedule. It felt like she was a walking pillbox at times.

"What's all this noise about?" came a rich African voice as Precious walked through the bedroom door, followed by Gloria, their beaming smiles and white teeth in marked contrast to David's glum expression.

"It's Mary. She's getting worse. I can't handle this any more," David replied.

Precious came round to his side of the bed and rubbed his arm. "I know it's hard, my love. We are here to look after both of you, isn't that right?" Precious said, looking across at her colleague. Precious and Gloria came in three times a day to look after Mary, but even that didn't seem to be enough these days. Where possible, they would dress her, make them breakfast, lunch, and dinner and attend to Mary's personal needs.

"Why don't you go downstairs and make yourself a cup of tea? Me and Gloria can look after Mary for a while and get her dressed," she said, placing her hand on the small of David's back and guiding him towards the bedroom door.

David's shoulders sagged as he dragged his weary feet across the carpet, not even bothering to glance over his shoulder as he made his way through the hallway and down the stairs. It was like this every day and, as each month passed, he was struggling to keep up with her demands. He couldn't go out much. It was too risky. He always got a food delivery from the local Sainsbury's and only headed out when he needed any essentials they had run out of. The local chemist delivered Mary's medicine once a month. He had done everything possible to make his routine hands-off, but it led to a very miserable existence.

David flicked on the kettle and grabbed the mug from the overhead unit before dropping a teabag into the empty cup and leaning against the kitchen worktop. He glanced round the space. No one had decorated the kitchen for years, and it needed a fresh coat of paint and updated units, but why bother? Mary wouldn't appreciate it, and he didn't have the time to sit back and admire it.

The kettle had been bubbling for what felt like minutes before the switch popped off. He turned round and poured the hot water into his cup and grabbed the spoon before spending the next few minutes stirring his teabag round the cup. He liked his tea dark and strong. Just a tiny splash of milk, something Mary hated. At least she couldn't spoil his daily cuppa any more by making her dishwater tea, which was weak, tasteless, and pale.

He sighed as he thought about his life. It had been non-existent for the past two years. Foolish decisions had not only put him in jeopardy but had ruined his marriage and forced a giant wedge between himself and Mary. The money hadn't made life any easier. It had made it harder.

He picked up his mug and sat at the dining table. Though there were six chairs, he sat in the same seat every day for breakfast, lunch, and dinner. He would sit alone and in silence, slowly chewing every mouthful to distract him from the boredom of his existence.

From the kitchen worktop, his mobile rang. David rolled his eyes before pushing his chair back and slowly rising to his feet and heading back into the kitchen.

Glancing at the screen, he nodded. It was Michael. "Hello there," David answered. He narrowed his eyes and pulled the phone away from his ear as loud music belted through the speaker. "What on earth?" he said, pulling the phone back towards his ear. He froze as he heard screaming on the other end of the line. Not the screaming from someone who was terrified, but the screams from someone in pain. Blood-curdling cries. "Michael? Is that you? What's happened?" The screams and crying continued before the line went dead. David pulled the phone away. His wide eyes stared at the blank screen of his phone in the palm of his hand.

A lump of fear burnt in his stomach. The lump began to grow and stretch, taking over his chest, throat, and then the rest of him until he felt like his body was going to burst into flames.

David's mind raced. What had happened to Michael? Was he hurt? Was he in danger? He picked up the phone and dialled Michael's number, but no one answered. He tried again, and still, nothing. Panic set in as he tried to make sense of the situation. He couldn't call 999. They'd ask too many questions, and they could trace his number. He couldn't risk the police turning up on his doorstep. Shit.

# 3

CREADY WAITED until the evening before stuffing Michael's body in the boot of the stolen Honda Jazz. He'd spent the entire afternoon tearing the house apart looking for the money, bank statements, or safe keys. He needed evidence to prove that Michael had or knew where the money was. Despite his thorough search, Cready couldn't find anything. He was sure that Michael knew more, but he hadn't caved in. Battered and bruised, Michael had remained defiant and pleaded his innocence until the very end. But his pleas fell on deaf ears. Cready wasn't interested in excuses. He'd heard them a thousand times over the years. Each victim begging for their life before he snuffed them out.

He'd ventured into the garden shed and turned everything upside down before heading back inside and rifling through every single cupboard and drawer, looking beneath beds, pulling up the corners of carpets, and searching the space under the stairs. He was certain he had left no inch of the house untouched. When the police finally arrived, they would assume it was a house burglary. Michael was nothing more than collateral damage, and, with his remains stuffed in the boot, Cready needed to get rid of him fast.

Cready headed to an industrial estate on the outskirts of town that he knew would be deserted at this time of night. He knew for certain because he'd driven the streets several times looking for the ideal spot, as well as checking when the estate fell silent. Speeding through the narrow streets, the tyres squealed and screeched as he threw the Jazz round the corners. He finally came to a halt at a dead end where the industrial estate stopped, and scrubland continued beyond the bollards. He switched off the engine and sat in the darkness for a few minutes, scoping the area and checking for any signs of movement. It was eerily quiet and deserted. Perfect.

Stepping from the car, he allowed his eyes to adjust to the environment before coming round to the boot and popping it open. Michael's body lay on its side, the man's knees pulled into his chest. Cready hauled the body out and exhaled deeply before dragging it to the open driver's door and dropping Michael's body into the seat, securing him with the driver's seat belt. After removing a few items from the carrier bag he'd brought with him, he tossed them into the boot. He was covering his tracks well, and the items would only confuse the police even further. Closing the boot, he opened the rear passenger door and retrieved the can of petrol, scattering its contents inside the cabin of the car, ensuring he soaked the seats before moving round to the front driver's side and doing it again.

Taking one last look to make sure everything was right, he pulled out a box of Swan matches from his jacket and struck one, letting the flame take hold before tossing it into Michael's lap, the combustion was instant, a wall of flames filling the cabin in seconds. The heat was so intense, Cready staggered back. The orange flames lit up his dark face as he glared at the fireball. He watched as the flames consumed the car, the crackling sound becoming louder as the fire spread, and thick black smoke billowed into the night sky. Cready stepped back, satisfied that Michael's body would be burnt beyond recognition. And by the time they did a dental record check, his work would be done anyway. This was about buying time.

He needed to make sure there was nothing left of Michael's remains, no trace that could lead the police to him. He felt the rush of adrenaline flood his body, a satisfying smirk tugging at his lips. It was done.

Cready was in no hurry to go as he pulled out Michael's phone from his back pocket and examined its photo gallery. He had removed the SIM card and left it at Michael's house. Michael had made the silly mistake of hanging on to a birthday card still in its envelope. It was postmarked in York. Pictures on his phone had the geolocation information stored in the metadata of each file. Michael had provided him with the precise location where the photographs were captured. Silly and careless on Michael's part, but a pure stroke of luck for Cready as he flicked through the images. The wall of flames grew stronger as an inferno engulfed the car. Yellow and golden flames pirouetting and dancing towards the sky.

He glanced down at the phone again and scrolled through some family pictures. The man he was looking for was still alive, and Michael had led him straight to the front door.

Michael's mistake made his job so much easier. He felt nothing. No anger, no sadness, or guilt. This was business. His line of business. He never spoke or expressed an opinion. They called him the Silent Assassin for a reason.

# 4

KAREN PULLED up behind the line of police vehicles and other emergency responders. It had been a long time since she'd been called out to a burnt-out vehicle. But this one had far more sinister implications. "A Honda Jazz? Hardly a prized car to nick," Karen joked as she looked at the mangled mess of metal.

Jade nodded. "Mercedes, BMW, Audi, or Range Rover. Then yes. The Honda Jazz, according to the reg, it was red, which I find hard to believe," Jade remarked, staring at the brown and grey metal smouldering skeleton.

Karen agreed. Cars were often stolen to be used in criminal activity, or by bored youths with nothing better to do. While back in uniform, she'd lost count of the number of high-speed pursuits where she'd ultimately discovered the occupants were under the age of sixteen. "But this is a Honda Jazz? It makes little sense?" Karen said as she got closer to the burnt-out remains. Izzy and SOCO were already in attendance as she spotted Izzy's flame-red hair among a group of people huddled close to the vehicle.

Seeing Karen approach, Izzy pulled herself away from the huddle.

"Morning, Karen. An interesting one for you today," she said, zipping up her jacket and pulling her hair out of a scrunchie.

"A burnt-out car is not a problem, but burnt human remains as well? I've seen enough to last a lifetime." Karen's mind wandered back to a recent case involving the arson attack and death of six members from the Lawson farming family. "What can you tell me?" Karen looked over Izzy's shoulder towards the car where fire service personnel were erecting screens round the remains to shield it from a growing number of people appearing from other parts of the industrial estate.

"Human remains in the driver's seat. Male. I can't tell you anything else. I can't give you an age or race. They could be black, white, or Asian. I'll have to do a more detailed examination once I have them on the table."

"It doesn't give us much to go on," Karen said, scratching her head as she turned towards Jade. "Can you see if we can get a VIN plate off the vehicle? We can run it through the DVLA and locate the owner's details. But here's the question. Is the owner in the vehicle or is it someone who nicked it and then set themselves alight? The latter of which makes little sense."

"Will do," Jade replied, heading off to speak to the fireman closest to the vehicle.

Bart Lynch, the CSI manager, came round from the other side of the burnt vehicle to join Karen as she approached.

"Hi, Karen. We are arranging for a low-loader to recover the vehicle so we can carry out a more thorough inspection at the workshop. It looks like they set the vehicle alight using petrol as the accelerant. There is a strong whiff of it where the back seats used to be."

Karen leaned over and peered into the rear passenger area to see nothing more than coiled springs vaguely resembling the outline of the seats. The intensity of the fire had blackened and twisted them, too. She came round to the driver's side and braced herself. The blackened and charred remains of the victim sat in the seat. Their mouth stretched open in a half-smile, providing a marked contrast to the white teeth against the blackened and taut skin. She glanced in. The metal clip from the seat belt sat in its housing. Though most of the seat belt fabric had burnt away, it confirmed the victim had been secured in their seat when the fire started. "The question on my mind, was it suicide? and if so, it's a bloody horrible way to go."

Bart shrugged. "I'm not sure at the moment. Izzy would be the best person to confirm whether the victim was dead or alive before the fire started. With the state of the remains, it's impossible for us to confirm whether the victim had sustained any injuries. I couldn't see any, especially any gunshot wounds or penetration points to the torso."

Karen looked over her shoulder to see Ed and Preet arrive.

"Morning, Karen," Ed said, doing up the button on his jacket.

"Morning, you two. Where's Ty?"

Ed rolled his eyes. "Ty was on a date last night. Taken today off."

"Dirty stop-out," Karen said. "I need you to make enquiries in the local units round here. Start with those closest to the scene. Find out if they have any CCTV overlooking this area. My guess is they haven't but, if they do, it's focused on the yards in front of the units. But you never know," Karen said.

"Sure, no problem."

Karen took a few moments to wander up and down the road. It was a typical industrial estate with units of varying sizes. Closest to her was a storage facility, a large workshop offering MOTs and car servicing, a manufacturer of plastic packaging and a timber merchant. She was thankful the flames hadn't sent plumes of hot embers towards the timber yard. Glancing further down the road, Karen noticed most of the other units were busy with staff milling round, vehicles arriving and other vehicles heading out on deliveries.

During the day, it was a hive of activity but, at night, these places took on a very sinister feeling. She remembered lurking in the shadows while unofficially staking out a suspect's industrial unit in an earlier case. Not a single person had passed her way and, with little to no traffic, such locations proved perfect for joyriders, courting couples, and drug dealers.

Karen stood on the edge of the pavement, hands on her hips as she thought about the route the Honda Jazz would have taken. There was one main road leading into the estate, with several smaller cut-throughs. The smell of fried food pulled her from her thoughts. A breakfast van parked a little further up the road. *Perfect timing*, she thought, as she hurried over. Grabbing a coffee and bacon butty, she took a slow walk back to the crime scene, savouring every large mouthful.

## 5

KAREN RETURNED to the office just after lunch. The investigation into the burnt-out wreckage was still ongoing, with several of Bart's team members still in attendance. They had brought a specialist team in to do a fingertip search of the area surrounding the vehicle and, so far, the results were less than encouraging in Karen's opinion.

"Right, team. Let's get your backsides round the whiteboard," Karen said, pinning up a few images of the burnt-out vehicle for everyone to see. "This is a bit of an unusual case, and we are treating it as a suspicious death. We were called to attend a burnt-out wreckage earlier this morning. It wasn't until the fire service brought the fire under control they discovered the body of what we now believe to be a male, sitting in the driver's seat." Karen pinned up further grizzly images of the burnt human remains.

"Any idea on the identity?" an officer asked.

Karen shook her head. "Early days yet. There were no personal effects on the victim, so it may be a while before we can identify who the poor sod was."

"I've got the VIN plate details and ran it through the DVLA," Jade said. "It was a red twenty-one plate Honda Jazz, stolen three nights ago in Manchester and registered to Anne Parish. I'll arrange for someone from the team to call her, and I've pulled the crime reference number off the system."

Karen folded her arms across her chest as she turned and looked back at the images. "Okay. Thanks, Jade. We need to identify the victim as well as decide whether they stole the car. Even if they did, why would they drive all the way to York and then set themselves and the car alight?"

"It's a pretty savage way to go," Dan remarked. "Surely there are quicker ways to take your own life than setting fire to yourself."

Karen agreed. Based on her time in the Met, the most common methods of suicide she had come across had been hanging, strangulation, and suffocation, all of which had continued to increase in recent years. Karen thought about a course she had taken about suicide awareness and prevention. As far as she could remember, all three methods combined, accounted for nearly sixty per cent of all suicides in England and Wales. And firearm, smoke, and fire deaths accounted for about five per cent. So, in her opinion, a crime like this was very rare.

"Izzy is doing the post-mortem tomorrow. I'm hoping she can extract a decent blood sample for DNA identification purposes. The victim's teeth appeared to be intact, so there's the possibility of doing a dental record check," Karen said.

"It's hard to know what his mental state was," Preet added. "Maybe he wanted to take his life but was in such a distressed state he just drove anywhere and ended up on our patch by chance. He could have been a tortured soul and wanted to suffer pain as some kind of punishment as he took his life? It's not unheard of."

Preet's comment had everyone sitting in silence, a few of them nodding as they processed her words.

"Quite possible, Preet," Karen nodded. "At the moment, most of this is speculation. We know who the car belonged to, so our next port of call is speaking to Anne Parish."

"There's nothing on the crime reference report to suggest she knew the person who stole her car," Jade said, glancing at the printout in her hand.

There were far too many unknowns in this case for Karen to be definite about anything. "Any joy with the CCTV trawl?" she asked, looking in Ed's direction.

"We spoke to all the units surrounding the scene. They all have CCTV, but only cover their buildings and their yards. A few cameras were pointed towards their entrances and those were the ones we grabbed footage from. Though I would point out, looking at their monitors, we may not see much."

"Anything is better than nothing, Ed. Review the footage and see if you can spot the Jazz arriving. We are probably looking at between eleven p.m. and four a.m. The fire service was called at four forty-nine a.m. when a manager of one unit arrived early to open up and saw the car alight.

There was nothing he could do because the flames were so intense. He wasn't even aware there was a body inside until we informed him a few hours later."

"When do you think we will get an update from forensics?" Ned asked.

"I'll be chasing Bart in the next few hours. I'm not sure how much evidential material will be remaining. Fire at a crime scene is our nemesis. We all remember how difficult it was to get forensic evidence at the Lawson's farm. I can't see this being any different. Any combustible material had perished in the fire." Karen tapped the images of the burnt-out vehicle. "As you can see, there is nothing inside other than the mess of tangled and twisted metal."

Karen paused for a moment. She tapped a finger on her chin as she mulled the situation over. "Can someone check misper records for any males reported missing in the Manchester area in the last three days? The victim may not have been from Manchester. He could have come from the surrounding areas and, in fact, from any part of the country. But let's start with Manchester before we extend our search. We can add further details to our victim profile once Izzy has performed the post-mortem. Anyone have anything else to add?" Karen asked, looking round the team. Her question was met with a few grumbles as several officers got to their feet. "Good. I'll update the Super."

# 6

KAREN CHECKED the time on her watch. She had promised to go to Zac's for dinner after he had offered to cook them both a meal this evening. Karen hadn't needed convincing. Zac was a far better cook than she ever was, and he made everything look so easy. He had mentioned on more than one occasion how he found preparing a meal so relaxing and a pleasant distraction away from work. Karen loved that about him. There was no fuss or drama with Zac. Other than his work, his focus was on being the best dad to Summer while also throwing his heart and soul into their flourishing relationship.

Much had changed for them in recent weeks. Her near-death experience at the hands of Professor Bryant had made her reassess her life. In the not so recent past, her job had been her life. She'd ripped through a string of drunken one-night flings to dull the stress and pain of such a high-stress and dangerous occupation. But when she met Zac, everything changed. Though she had been nervous to open up in the beginning, she had learned to trust him, and the more she did, the deeper she fell in love with him. A sense of vulnerability melted away each time she lay in his arms, and in a funny way she felt she had grown up since coming to York. Zac was her everything, and he brought the balance into her life.

As she thought about him, her heart ached. An overwhelming urge to grab her bag and dash out of the office washed over her with every mental image. She smiled as she looked at the time. It wouldn't be long before she could leave.

"Karen, am I interrupting?" Ed asked, appearing in the doorway.

Karen laughed. "No, not at all. What's up?"

"A few of us have been looking through the CCTV footage from the industrial units close to the crime scene over the last few hours. We've spotted the Jazz from one camera angle. There's only a few seconds of footage and it's not clear, but there was just one occupant in the car."

Karen sat up, her eyes wide in surprise. "Seriously? It's definitely our car?"

Ed shrugged his shoulder and nodded. "We think so. We spotted the headlights and wheels of another three cars between eleven p.m. and two a.m. They were ruled out when we checked them against another camera. The Jazz drove past at three seventeen a.m. heading towards the dead end."

Karen jumped up from her chair, desperate to see the footage for herself. She followed Ed to the interview room before dropping into a seat in front of the monitor with Ed beside her. Ed rolled the footage to three seventeen a.m.

where Karen saw the Honda Jazz drive past. The footage wasn't clear enough for any identification purposes, but she saw the outline of one figure in the car. "So the driver killed themselves?"

"Well, this is the interesting point. We continued playing the footage for over an hour. No one else travelled back in the direction of where the car had come from. But we've checked with the council CCTV control room. They have one camera looking out over the scrubland beyond the bollards. After repeated fly-tipping and complaints about homeless people sleeping there, they installed a camera and luckily for us we caught a glimpse of someone walking through the scrub and away from the scene, but we only saw their legs because of the angle of the camera."

Karen thumped her fist on the table. "Bummer. I can't imagine they knew there was a camera there because if they did they would have avoided the area completely. I think by sheer luck and chance they avoided being seen."

"They might be a suspect. What if this individual met the victim at the scene and then murdered them? Why not contact the emergency services if they were not connected?" Ed asked as he jabbed a finger at the screen.

"You might be right, Ed. This puts a whole new slant on the investigation. The scene may have been staged to look like a horrendous suicide, or the legs captured on the council footage may belong to a homeless bod just wandering through who wanted to keep themselves to themselves. They're suspicious of the authorities at the best of times and might chose to turn a blind eye to any suspicious activity. Okay, can you print off a few copies for us and then send this footage to the high-tech unit and put in a request for an enhancement of the occupant in the vehicle?"

"Of course. Anything else?" Ed asked.

"Can you get down to the industrial estate tomorrow and take a few extra members of the team with you? Work back from the crime scene to the main entrance to the industrial estate and stop at every unit to grab a copy of their CCTV. We need a better angle on the car." Karen's mind shifted into overdrive as excitement bubbled inside her. "You should hopefully find CCTV on the main road leading into the estate. Check online to see if there are any cameras in the area and get on to the council control room to find out what coverage they have. We need to find out which direction the vehicle travelled from."

"Do you think it's come straight from Manchester? Someone stole the car three days ago."

"I don't know, is my honest answer, Ed. We have to build a timeline of where the vehicle was. It is possible that someone stored the vehicle somewhere, or used it in Manchester, and then brought it to York in the early hours of the morning. Can you do me a favour and get on to Manchester Council's CCTV room? Find out if they've picked up the vehicle on their cameras through ANPR. If so, it might help us figure out where the vehicle was before landing up on our patch."

Karen rose from her chair and headed for the door, buoyed by the news. "Well done, Ed."

# 7

CREADY SAT low down in a new stolen vehicle, parked not far from his target's house. With painstaking patience, he'd waited for hours as the sun dipped below the horizon. Darkness was his ally, allowing him to blend into the shadows as he watched and waited.

It hadn't taken him long to locate the street. Michael's carelessness had unwittingly saved him valuable time. Walking up and down the street had helped him narrow down the house. On his camera roll, there was a picture of Michael and the man he sought, arms casually slung over each other's shoulders—a glaring mistake for someone trying to stay hidden.

Jobs like this demanded both patience and certainty. His clients paid him for results, with little room for error. This was his second visit of the day, having been here at lunchtime as well. The street wasn't busy, which complicated his task. There was a risk that a vigilant neighbour might call the police if they grew suspicious.

He needed absolute certainty that it was the right house. His earlier position hadn't offered a direct line of sight. When two women in a little Corsa, dressed in light blue tunic tops and navy trousers, pulled up and stepped out, he couldn't tell who had opened the door for them. Correcting his mistake, he parked closer to the property, nestled between two cars, with a clear view of the front door. He glanced at his phone to check the time, realising he had been waiting in this spot for two hours. It didn't take long before his diligence bore fruit. The Corsa pulled up again, and the same two women emerged, engrossed in conversation, their laughter echoing down the street, a sign of their amusement.

This presented an opportunity to confirm if Harman's target was inside. The women approached the front door in a leisurely manner, before one of them rang the doorbell. Cready sat up in his seat, eyes fixed on the front door. It took a moment, but the door finally swung open, revealing an elderly gentleman. He watched as the man stepped aside to let the ladies pass through. They exchanged words, but Cready was too far away to catch their conversation. He reached for his phone, scrolling through his photo gallery until he found the image he needed. His attention shifted between the picture and the man standing in the open doorway.

Satisfied, he tapped out a message into WhatsApp.

*Your person is found. Identity confirmed.*

He pressed send and waited for the message to be delivered. The two ticks confirmed the delivery, and after a few moments, they turned blue to confirm that the recipient had read the message. He saw the recipient typing a reply, which came through a few seconds later.

*Excellent. Send him my regards and wish him a safe journey on my behalf.*

Stuffing the phone back in his jacket, he continued to stare at the house. The women were carers who had spent forty-five minutes at the house over lunchtime. He wondered if they were there for him or his wife. Perhaps he couldn't care for himself any more and needed extra help, or his wife was bedridden. Either way, it didn't matter to Cready, though he preferred the second scenario because she would be out of the way.

He placed one hand on the wheel and tapped his index finger slowly, one tap every five seconds. It was another one of his rituals he carried out before every job. It helped to slow his heartbeat and quell any surge of adrenaline. The carers reappeared forty minutes later, both waving in a jolly manner at the man as they trundled back up the drive towards the car. His target lingered in the doorway, not reciprocating the gesture nor engaging in any conversation.

*Perhaps he's a miserable bastard.*

A further few minutes passed before the car pulled away and disappeared down the road. He took a slow deep breath and let the air escape before zipping up his jacket and stepping out of the car. He needed to act fast.

# 8

"I THOUGHT you'd never get here," Zac said, wrapping his arms round Karen and kissing her softly.

Karen buried her head in his chest and enjoyed the warmth of his body against hers. Every time she stood there in his embrace it felt like nothing else mattered. The stress and worries of the day melted away and left her feeling sleepy and relaxed. "I know. I'm really sorry. The case we've just taken on took a sudden and dramatic turn this afternoon."

"The body in the burnt-out car? I heard a few officers speculating it might have been suicide?"

Karen took off her jacket and hung it on the newel post before kicking off her shoes and following Zac into the kitchen. Though she had her own apartment to go to, it never felt as homely or relaxing as when she was here and yet, strangely, she had spent the last few years living alone and enjoying her own space. The solitude she experienced in the apartment felt like a cold emptiness and one she wasn't comfortable with. Perhaps it was the fact she'd never had the perfect happy home because Karen's parents spent so much time caring for her disabled sister, which left little time for her.

"Wine?"

"Do you really need to ask?" Karen replied, rolling her eyes.

Zac shrugged as if he had asked a silly question. He poured a large white for her and topped up his own glass.

"On first impression it looked like a nasty suicide. Someone who was so troubled they picked one of the most horrendous ways to take their own life. I don't think I've ever attended a suicide by fire in my entire career, which is why I found this one so odd."

"There are easier ways to take your life," Zac remarked.

Karen nodded. "I know, right?" Karen took a hefty glug of wine and savoured the sharpness as it tickled her taste buds. She closed her eyes and groaned in pleasure, enjoying the moment. "Anyway, while the team was doing a CCTV trawl, Ed identified the Jazz and one occupant, as well as an individual walking away from the scene. If they were innocent, they would have seen the car on fire. The bollards and scrubland are just yards from our scene, and they could have dialled 999."

Zac's eyes widened. "Oh. It puts a whole new slant on the investigation."

"Exactly. The individual might have lured our victim to the spot and killed them before burning the vehicle."

His brow furrowed as he thought about it. "Maybe they didn't want to get involved?"

Karen shrugged. It was a possibility.

"Drugs feud? Maybe one of the foot soldiers was ripping off the OCG, and this was his punishment? They stole the car from Manchester, right?"

Karen nodded.

"Manchester has a massive drug problem. You only need to look at the Cheetham Hill area to understand the scale of it. One of the major OCGs actively moves firearms and wholesale amounts of cocaine and heroin throughout the UK. It wasn't long ago they were moving firearms down to Bedfordshire. Luton, I think," Zac said, staring at the ceiling as he recalled the facts.

Karen leaned against the worktop counter as she pondered Zac's comment. "We are liaising with our Manchester counterparts on the stolen vehicle. I might speak to one of the DCIs there to understand the current state of play."

Zac took a sip of his wine. "It's worth keeping your options open. There was another gang operating in Manchester city centre. I can't remember the details precisely, but about eighteen months ago one of the junior members of the OCG had shot off his mouth about the gang's activities. He was found a few days later with his tongue cut out and acid poured over the groin area of his jeans. It melted his dick and bollocks. He's still alive, but he'll be drinking through a straw and pissing through a plastic tube for the rest of his life."

Karen winced as she crunched up her eyes. "Jesus. That's savage."

"I know. Your victim might have been on the receiving end of a punishment order handed down to him by the principal members of an OCG. It certainly serves as a deterrent to other members of the gang, don't you think?" Zac suggested as he pulled out a chopping board and retrieved the vegetables and chicken from the fridge.

"Interesting. I'll bear it in mind. What I need to find from Izzy tomorrow is whether our victim was dead or alive before they started the fire."

"That's enough about work. How about we sort out the dinner and then, if you're not too tired, catch a movie on Prime?" Zac suggested.

Karen smiled as she put down her wine glass and stepped over towards Zac, wrapping her arms round his waist. "How can I resist? Dinner, wine, movie, and a gorgeous man." Karen kissed him. "Right, what can I do?"

"I'll do the chicken, and you can do the vegetables? We can stick it all on a tray and shove it in the oven."

"Sounds perfect. Where is Summer this evening?"

Zac shrugged. "She's out with Lottie and a few friends. I imagine they are hanging round outside the chip shop in town. Hang on, let me check," Zac said, reaching for his phone and finding the Find My app to locate Summer's phone. "Yep, chip shop."

"Zac, can I ask a favour? Considering I'm here *often*, could we keep Manky here? At least he won't be on his own so much, and I'm sure Summer would be happy to have him round. Please be honest, if you don't think it's right, then say so. Don't worry about offending me, just tell me what you think."

"Is this your way of staying here permanently?" Zac teased.

Karen burst out laughing as her cheeks blushed. "That's not what I said. I think the last thing you want is another woman living under this roof," she said, almost hoping Zac would disagree with her.

"I'm only teasing. I haven't got an issue with it and Summer would *definitely* not have a problem with it. She's always gone on about us having a dog or cat. You're right, you wouldn't need to rely on your neighbours to keep checking on him and he seems harmless."

Karen's heart pounded in her chest. She wanted to cry tears of happiness, but knew she would look like a sap, and it would be hard to explain why she felt so emotional. "You're amazing. He's going to love it here. I can't wait to tell him."

Zac let out a chuckle. "He's a cat, Karen. He doesn't understand most of the things you say to him. Manky is hardly going to be jumping for joy and rushing to pack his bags when you tell him he's moving here!"

"Manky understands everything. He has feelings like all animals. He picks up on my vibe. So if I'm excited, he gets excited too. I guess you've never had a pet while growing up?"

"A hamster. Does that count?"

Karen tutted and rolled her eyes before pointing an accusatory finger in his direction. "You'd better be nice to him, or you could end up with a splash of Domestos on your boxer shorts during the night!"

"Ouch."

They continued cooking and their tongue-in-cheek slanging match, before eating and then curling up in each other's arms. Life had never been so good, and Karen was relishing every second.

## 9

CREADY STEPPED out of the car and glanced up and down the street. It was quiet. No dog walkers and no cars. The quicker he got on with the job the sooner he could leave and get paid. He went round to the boot and retrieved a hi-vis jacket and clipboard. Slipping the yellow jacket over his own, and with a clipboard in one hand, he headed over towards the property, pausing for a moment to take one last look up and down the street before venturing down the path and ringing the doorbell.

He was a man of few words who preferred to get on with the job, but this one required a little extra. It was a few moments before the door was answered by the same elderly man he had seen before.

"Sorry to disturb you. I'm an engineer with Npower. We've had reports of power outages in the area and we're checking with elderly residents to make sure they are okay. Is all your electricity working?" Cready asked.

The elderly man looked tired and flustered. He muttered something incomprehensible and then shook his head.

"Sorry?" Cready asked.

The man tutted. "Everything is fine here."

"That's good to hear. Can you do me a quick favour and check your fuse box to make sure none of the circuits have tripped? I'll wait outside if that's okay?"

"Is that necessary?" the man asked.

"I want to make sure. If a fuse has tripped, I can arrange for one of our engineers to test your circuits and make sure there are no faults. The last thing we want is your kettle shorting out and causing a small electrical fire."

*Casting doubt and the risk of fire alarmed most people and is a useful ploy.*

The old man shook his head. "Wait here a moment." He closed the gap in the door, leaving it on the latch before disappearing into the hallway.

Cready edged the door open and stepped into the hallway, closing the door behind him as he watched the old man open the door under the stairs and switch on the lights. Cready came up behind him and threw his hand over the old man's mouth, dragging him backwards into the lounge. The man was too weak and frail to defend himself as he lost his footing and collapsed backwards. Cready threw the old man on to the sofa and towered over him.

The man whimpered and cried in confusion. "Take what you need. Don't hurt me. We haven't got much."

Cready stepped forward and placed his hand round the old man's neck. "That's not what I've heard. Where is the money?"

"What money? Look, my wallet is on the table. There's twenty quid in there. Take it. I have nothing else," the old man pleaded.

"You're lying. My client wants his money back. You have two choices. You can tell me where the money is and you won't get hurt, or I can hurt you so much you will bleed to death slowly and wish you had chosen the first option."

The man shook his head and cowered as he fought for a breath. "I don't know what you're talking about. What money? I haven't got much in the bank. I've got a few thousand pounds in savings. That's it. You can have it. I'll give you my bank details."

"Who is it?" came a woman's voice from somewhere upstairs. "Is that you, Stephen?" she shouted.

Cready stared at the ceiling and smiled. "You're coming with me," Cready growled as he grabbed the old man off the sofa by the collar of his pyjamas and forced him up the stairs. The old man tumbled as he lost his footing, his face landing on one step. He let out a muffled yell as he threw his hands to his face. He sobbed as his shoulders shook.

"Get up. We haven't started yet," Cready hissed as he stepped over the old man and grabbed him by the back of his pyjama top and hauled him up the last few steps before dragging him into the bedroom.

The woman sat there looking alarmed and stared on in silence, the fingers on her left hand pulling on her bottom lip. "Are you Stephen?" she asked. "He always comes to say hello and brings me a cup of tea."

"Shut up," Cready said, jabbing a finger in her direction. He turned towards the man and pulled him up before dropping him into a chair in the corner of the bedroom. He punched the man in the face, splitting the translucent skin across his cheekbone. Blood trickled down his cheek. "I'll ask you again, where is the money?"

The man shook his head, a dazed and pained expression on his face as his eyes rolled about in their sockets.

Cready looked round and saw a discarded sock on the floor. He picked it up and jammed it into the man's mouth before grabbing the bony right index finger and twisting it, the fragile bone snapping with little effort. A muffled howl filled the room. "I need an answer. There are plenty more fingers to break." The man quivered as Cready grabbed the next finger.

The man shook his head, his eyes fixed wide in terror and pain.

"Wrong answer." Cready struck the old man across the face with the back of his hand. The cold, hard slap made the old man sob like a child.

Cready wasn't having any of it and pulled out his tin snips from the inside of his jacket. He placed the jaws round the right pinky finger and brought the blades down through the soft skin and thin bone. A crack. The digit dropped to the floor as the old man jerked back in agony as bolts of pain raced up his arm.

"I'll ask you one last time. What have you done with the money?"

The man slid down in the chair; his head tipped back in shock as his mouth hung open.

*Looks like I'll have to find it myself.*

Cready noticed the old woman hadn't moved. She was still playing with her bottom lip. As he stepped in her direction, she flinched.

"Are you Stephen?" she asked again.

"Who gives a shit?" he replied, pulling the cord from her dressing gown and heading back towards the man. Looping the cord round the old man's neck, he tightened it. The old man thrashed in the chair, clawing at the ligature. His legs flailed as his heels dug into the carpet. Spittle flew from his lips as his throat gurgled.

In mere moments, his life faded away like the last ember of a dying fire, leaving behind only a battered and vacant husk slumped in the chair.

## 10

KAREN PARKED in the hospital car park and waited for Ed. A recent text from him confirmed he was only minutes away, which gave Karen the opportunity to catch up with her emails and WhatsApp messages.

The first email was from her team on the car from Manchester. Anne Parish had reported her car as stolen when she'd woken in the morning. She was in possession of her car keys, so someone had bypassed the ignition system. Upon reviewing the report, Manchester city's control room had begun to search for the stolen Jazz. The review of footage had picked up the Jazz on ANPR cameras in three locations over the course of the next twenty-four hours, but they'd been unable to offer a clear image of the person driving. The review of their footage would continue. At least Karen could be certain the car had remained in Manchester for at least one of the three days before being discovered in York.

It wasn't the news Karen had been hoping for and the disappointment continued when Manchester police confirmed no missing person reports were filed in the three days between the Honda Jazz being stolen and it being found burnt out. If it was a gang member who'd met their death, then Karen wondered if someone would ever report their disappearance because many of the gang members came from broken homes.

As she continued to scroll, another email piqued Karen's interest. It was a summary from Bart Lynch, the CSI manager. They'd been unable to recover any useful forensic evidence in the car. However, upon freeing the boot mechanism, they'd discovered an axe, knife, and knuckleduster. Karen scrunched up her nose. They weren't common items you would find in a car, and Anne Parish confirmed they didn't belong to her. Karen thought back to her conversation with Zac the night before regarding the organised crime scene in Manchester. She could lend more weight to his theory of it being a punishment killing of a gang member who'd crossed the line. The weapons recovered were like those often found discreetly hidden among gang members or in their vehicles.

Tap, tap, came the sound on her window.

Karen jumped in her seat when she saw Ed beside her door. She put the phone away and stepped out of the car. "Sorry, I didn't see you arrive."

"That's okay. I couldn't see your car at first, so walked round for a bit. Ready?"

Karen nodded and filled Ed in on the emails as they walked through the hospital towards the mortuary.

One of Izzy's assistants showed them in and gave them gowns to wear before leading them to the main examination room. The sound of *All Night Long* by Lionel Richie played on the radio as Karen walked in. She couldn't help but smile. Izzy had an eclectic taste in music, and what they would hear each time they arrived was very much pot luck. It could be anything from classical music, to rock, to R & B, and even a bit of country and western thrown in for good measure. Izzy was nodding her head to the music, looking up as Karen approached.

She greeted them with a beaming smile, and her eyes lit up, even though her mask puffed up every time she spoke.

Karen thought Izzy should bottle her enthusiasm and zest for life and sell it. She would make a fortune even in the most difficult of times.

"Morning, Izzy." Karen averted her eyes from the cadaver for a few moments while she acclimatised herself to the room, concentrating her efforts on staring at Izzy. Ed stood beside the table staring down at the charred and blackened remains.

"I've got so much on today, I started without you," Izzy said.

Karen shrugged. "Fine by me. I'd rather not see it at all. I've seen my fair share of blackened remains recently."

Izzy nodded. "Me too, but it needs to be done. I thought it'd be ages until I saw another deep-fried wonton and crispy body!"

Karen rolled her eyes at Izzy's black humour. Not able to put it off any longer, she took a deep breath and turned her gaze towards the cadaver. The body was contorted and stripped of all its identity. Normally a victim of a fire would find their limbs contracting, and their arms lifted in the classic pugilistic pose, but on this occasion, the seat belt had held the victim in place, so there was little evidence of contraction of the arms.

Karen sniffed the air. The lingering stench tugged at her memories, instantly transporting her to a previous case where the Lawson farming family died in an arson attack on their home. The complexity of the aroma was hard to describe. It reminded Karen of burnt beef mixed with the stench of burnt hair and the metallic smell and taste of coagulated blood. After tossing in the acrid smell of burnt plastic, that was as close as she could get to describing it. Visually, it was horrible. The smell was sickening. And the taste would take a while to leave her mouth.

Karen wrinkled her lip. "What can you tell us?"

"Well, if you were thinking this was someone in their teens or twenties or even thirties, then you would be sadly mistaken. We are looking at an elderly man, probably sixty-five years or older, based on bone density. He's missing three teeth, so we need a dental record check, and he has a pacemaker." Izzy turned towards a metal counter behind them. "The pacemaker is over there. The manufacturer and identification details are on it."

"I wasn't expecting that," Karen replied, shocked. "Brilliant. That gives us a lot to go on."

Turning to Ed she directed, "Ed, grab the details of the pacemaker and call the team. Get someone to chase up on those details. The identification number will be linked to the recipient."

Ed nodded and walked round the table with notepad and pen in hand.

The mounting evidence didn't match up with Izzy's observations. After reviewing the email from Bart Lynch, why would someone in their sixties own a knife, axe and knuckleduster? How could an elderly man be connected to them if this was gang-related? Perhaps the victim had fallen foul of them? Had he seen their activities and grassed on them? The gang dishing out their own form of punishment and revenge? Questions swirled round Karen's mind. Though it felt overwhelming, it also meant they were making progress.

"The pacemaker should save you a lot of time," Izzy remarked. "Normally in a case like this I'd have to rely on various techniques to decide the age of the victim such as assessments of the extent of cranial suture closure, parietal thinning, pubic symphysis metamorphosis, development of the sternal rib ends and the list goes on," she groaned. "Don't even get me started on checking for osteoarthritis, overall degenerative changes, changes to the auricular area and acetabulum of the pelvis, as well as dental and bone histology features. Some of which need the help of experts."

Karen laughed, not understanding half of the terms Izzy had used. "Cause of death? Or is that a silly question?" she asked, looking down at the taut blackened skin, which took on a slight sheen under the lights of the room.

"Crushing to the trachea. Strangulation."

Karen looked confused. "Wait, so, he was dead before the fire started?"

Izzy nodded. "Confirmed. There was no evidence of soot or heat damage to the trachea or lungs."

"That puts a new slant on the investigation."

"I'm sure it does. You may also be interested to hear he's missing the little finger on his right hand," Izzy added, lifting the hand for Karen to see.

From the damage to the end of the digit and the exposed bone and skin, it was a recent wound. Karen thanked Izzy for her time and looked forward to reading the full report.

## 11

ARRIVING BACK AT THE STATION, Karen made her way to the high-tech unit in search of an update following her request for video footage enhancement. Derek, a specialist, was responsible for cleaning up the footage as best as possible. After asking one of the first officers she came to, they directed her towards Derek's desk.

"Derek?" Karen asked as she stopped beside him.

The man pushed back in his chair and looked up at Karen, pushing the glasses from the bridge of his nose on to his forehead and rubbing his eyes. He had a long brown ponytail, a blue check shirt, and faded chinos. The combination offered little to enhance his image of a university geek who probably spent more time in front of a computer than drinking in the union bar.

Two big twenty-four-inch monitors took up most of his desk and an array of small digital boxes appeared to be plugged into the back of them.

"Yes, that's me. How can I be of help?" he replied, extending his hand.

He was well spoken and not what she had imagined, which took Karen by surprise. And thinking about it now, personified the kind of individual on *University Challenge* being questioned by Jeremy Paxman!

"Oh, hi. I'm DCI Karen Heath. You're reviewing footage for my team," Karen said, shaking his hand.

"Right. Yes. The CCTV footage taken from the industrial estate and the Honda Jazz, correct?" he asked for confirmation.

Karen nodded.

"I've got good and bad news. The footage is HD quality, and if the footage had been taken during the day, we would have a clear description for you. However, as with most CCTV footage, it's of inferior quality at night. Add the distance, and you're left with footage that's average," he said with a shrug of his shoulder.

"Is that the good or bad news?" she asked.

"That's the bad. The good news is we can't make out the face, but we can confirm the driver has dark skin," Derek added, wiggling his mouse and retrieving the relevant file for Karen to review.

Karen grimaced as she stared at the still images.

"Without adequate street lighting the footage was dark and grainy. It left little for us. There are three main types of night vision technologies used in CCTV cameras. These include infrared illumination, also known as active night vision, low-light amplification, also known as passive night vision, and thermal imaging," Derek explained. "Most CCTV cameras on the industrial estate are using infrared illumination. You may have noticed tiny LEDs round the lens of the security cameras, which act as a kind of floodlight which bathes the scene in front of the camera in infrared light. The camera's sensor, which is capable of detecting infrared light, will capture the intensity of the reflected light from the scenery and convert it into a video signal. Then, the signal gets enhanced and amplified by the camera to create a high-quality video. The limiting factor in this video footage," Derek said, pointing to the screen, "is the distance between the camera and the road. It's just too far for us to get a clear enough image. The further I enhance the image, the more pixilated it becomes. It's the best I can do for you. I'm really sorry."

Derek sounded truly apologetic, as if he had let Karen down.

"I appreciate your help on this, Derek. You have done the best you can. We are talking of at least sixty or seventy feet between the camera and the road. Maybe more. I guess there are limitations to the technology the cameras use."

"Sadly, yes. The only thing I would say came out of the review are rudimentary details about the driver. They had defined features. I would suggest someone in their thirties or forties."

Karen leaned over Derek's desk and peered at the image. It was noticeable, and the harder she looked the more she agreed. There appeared to be a sharp jawline. Her mind whirred. The victim may not have been the driver after all.

"Okay. Thank you, Derek. Can you send those enhanced images through to my email for me, please?"

"Of course."

## 12

KAREN RUSHED BACK to the SCU, keen to update the team.

"Okay, listen up. There's a small breakthrough in the CCTV clean-up. As we know, there was one occupant of the vehicle. The high-tech unit enhanced the image. The driver is likely to be dark-skinned, IC3, 4, or 6. According to Izzy, the victim was dead before the fire." Karen confirmed the sighting of an individual walking away from the scene.

"The victim was taken by car, and then disposed of?" Ned added. "And the individual seen walking away might have been the driver?"

Karen shrugged. "As yet, I'm unsure, but it's likely. No one else was spotted walking close to the scene, nor were there any other cars seen at the time of the fire. It's still unclear why someone set an elderly man on fire."

"Karen," one of her officers interrupted, "SOCO hasn't been able to retrieve any prints from the items found in the

Jazz's boot. There are scratches and dents on the axe and knife, but nothing else. The fire removed any evidence."

"Okay, thanks," Karen said as Belinda came through the doors of the SCU and joined the meeting.

"Perfect timing. I chased up the manufacturers and identification number on the pacemaker Ed phoned through," Bel said. "According to my notes, they fitted the device to a Michael Armstrong. Aged seventy-six, a retired pharmacist. No previous. We're compiling everything we can on him."

"Great, thanks. We have an address?" Karen asked.

Bel nodded. "Yes. An address in Haworth, one mile north of the city centre. It's quite a popular area with lots of sleepy streets, tree-lined verges, and a large population of elderly residents."

"Great. You and Ed can come with me to the address. Can you arrange for officers to attend with a big red key or get a locksmith? Whichever is quickest."

Bel grabbed her jacket and bag, making a few calls as she followed Karen out of the building.

---

IT TOOK a few minutes to arrive at the address. It was as Belinda had described. A quiet, leafy street with well-presented semi-detached properties, smart driveways, and small neatly manicured lawns hemmed in with hedges. Karen spotted a patrol car as she arrived. Two officers exited as she got out of her car.

Karen skirted round the black Vauxhall Astra parked in the drive and peered in through the front window, cupping her hands round her eyes to block out the glare. Her view set off alarm bells. She returned to the team. "Take in the door," Karen said, taking a few steps back.

One of the uniformed officers went back to his patrol car and retrieved the big red key from his boot. The key was a sizeable tool used as a quick entry method. The officer swung back and aimed it at the UPVC door. The door remained firm despite his second attempt to swing the big red key at it. Following several further unsuccessful attempts, Karen called in a locksmith. It took a further twenty minutes for someone to arrive, so Karen used the time waiting in her car to catch up with her team on any developments. She noticed a few residents beginning to appear at the edge of the gardens to see what was happening. Most of them were sixty plus, in Karen's opinion. Bel had already mentioned it was a safe area and popular with retirees. With supermarkets close by and a short drive into town, they could enjoy the luxury of a quieter life with the hustle and bustle of the city centre minutes away. The team regathered once the locksmith arrived and, after a few minutes of picking the lock, they were free to enter the property.

"Hello, it's the police!" Karen shouted as she ventured down the hallway. "Hello, is anyone here?"

Karen stepped into the lounge to find it in total disarray. Someone had opened the drawers and emptied them out on the floor. Cushions from the sofas lay torn apart. The sofa bases were turned upside down, and the carpets beneath them turned up at the corners. "Jesus, someone has really done a number here," she remarked.

"Same in the kitchen," Belinda added. The two uniformed officers were upstairs and confirmed the bedrooms were in a similar state. Every item of soft furnishing had been cut open. Every cupboard or drawer had been emptied. The loft hatch was open, with storage boxes scattered across the boarded floor.

"See this, Karen," Belinda said, standing next to the dining table towards the rear of the property. A dining chair lay on its side with loose pieces of rope still entangled in the legs. Evidence of blood was visible on the rope, chair, and the surrounding laminate floor. It wasn't the disturbed scene which troubled Karen, but a shrivelled finger on the floor.

Karen didn't step closer for fear of contaminating the area. "Bel, call SOCO. Let's pull back. We need to preserve the scene," Karen instructed.

They reconvened in the garden as further residents appeared, a look of concern on their faces. A female resident Karen imagined being in her sixties crossed from the front of her property and hovered in the driveway where they were standing. "Is everything okay? We haven't seen Michael today."

Karen joined the elderly resident. "Did you hear or see anything at Michael's house in the last twenty-four to thirty-six hours?"

The woman rested her fingers on her chin. Her eyes darted from Karen to the house and back to Karen. "No. I heard nothing that alarmed me. Why? What's happened?"

"We believe Michael may have come to harm."

The woman gasped and placed a hand over her mouth, visibly moved. "Oh, no. Oh, dear. Wh… what happened to him?"

"Unfortunately, I'm unable to give you further details at the moment. The investigation is in its early stages."

"Of course. I understand. Terrible news. Just terrible," she said. She turned and hurried back to her neighbours, who had gathered outside her house.

Karen rejoined her team and turned towards the two uniformed officers. "Can you start door-to-door enquiries and find out if anyone heard or saw anything unusual? Grab any doorbell and CCTV footage from neighbouring properties. Don't say anything about the discovery. The press team needs to release the information first, hopefully today."

They both nodded before splitting up and heading in different directions.

"Bel, can you get a few bodies from our team down here to help?"

"Sure." Bel shook her head as she glanced over the road at the small huddle of neighbours deep in discussion. "It doesn't make sense, Karen. Someone attacked, held, tortured, and murdered a seventy-six-year-old retired pharmacist before removing and taking his body to the industrial estate and setting him alight in a stolen vehicle."

Karen looked at the property and narrowed her eyes. "None of it makes sense."

## 13

THE TEAM GATHERED round Bel's desk following the gruesome discovery at Michael Armstrong's house. Karen perched on the end of the desk and shuffled through her papers.

Spotting Ty back at his desk, Karen couldn't resist the opportunity to wind him up. "Ah, so you honoured us with your presence today, Ty?" All eyes turned to Ty, who smiled sheepishly. "So what was the name of the poor girl who fell for your cringy one-liner?"

Ty let out an uncomfortable laugh.

"Wait…" Karen said, holding up a hand. "You found out her name, right?"

"Her name was… Um, no, wait!" Ty said, springing to his own defence.

His fellow officers fell about laughing as Ty squirmed in his chair. Taunts of "player!" were thrown in his direction.

"I'm sure she was lovely and felt sorry for you," Karen added.

Karen waited for the ripples of laughter to die down and threw a wink in Ty's direction. "Right. Shall we crack on? Where shall we start?"

Preet gestured that she had something to say. "Michael Armstrong is a retired pharmacist. He's originally from York, but has lived in Derby, Manchester, and Middlesbrough. From what I can gather, he was living and working in those towns during his career."

*There it is again. Another link to Manchester.*

"A widower," Preet continued. "His wife died four years ago, heart attack. He has a son in the US. We are trying to contact him. He has one brother, but we've been unable to locate him so far. I'll dig deeper."

"Anything financial?" Jade asked.

Turning in her seat, Preet glanced at Jade. "He has a NatWest account. Thirty-seven grand in savings, and a current account with just over eleven grand in it. He has a credit card, but there's nothing on it and he doesn't have any outstanding loans or debts."

"It may not have been a debt-related issue?" another officer speculated.

"It doesn't look like he was short of money," Karen replied. "Preet, let me know if you find anything else, and find out who his phone provider is. I want a copy of his call history for the last few weeks."

"What's the theory behind the pinky finger being lopped off?" Ty asked, wiggling the little finger on his right hand.

"I'm not sure to be honest," Karen replied. "I've seen it before in London, especially in gangland beatings. They'd lop off a finger as punishment or to get their victim to talk. DNA analysis should confirm if the digit belongs to him."

"I can't imagine a seventy-six-year-old retired pharmacist having gangland connections?" Ty added.

"Me neither," Karen said, turning to look at Michael Armstrong's picture pinned to the whiteboard.

"Mistaken identity?" Ty said.

Karen nodded. "Possible. It's not unheard of. But the Manchester angle bothers me. He worked in Manchester during a part of his career. The car he was found in was stolen from Manchester. Coincidence or intentional? We need another chat with our Manchester colleagues. Are we missing something?"

"Even if there is a Manchester connection, Michael worked there years ago. If there was a problem with his time there, then surely it would have surfaced before he retired and while he was still in Manchester?" an officer suggested.

"Agreed," Karen said. "Unless he left the area before whatever happened blew up and it's only caught up with him now. With the crazy way his assailant turned the house over, they were obviously looking for something. What did he have that someone wanted so badly? There must be more in his background than we are aware of. We need to find it. Crime scene investigators are combing through the property at the moment. I hope they find something."

Jade tapped the end of her pen on her notepad. "Illegal supply of medicines? There have been cases in the past of pharmacists selling hundreds of thousands of prescription-only medicines on the black market like diazepam and tramadol purchased from wholesalers and then later sold on to drug dealers." Jade paused as she recalled further details before continuing. "I remember a case in Bow, East London where a pharmacist initially sold medicines voluntarily to drug dealers. Later, he was forced to sell more medicines after the drug dealers threatened him outside his pharmacy."

A few officers tutted in disgust.

Jade recalled further details. "I think if I'm not mistaken, the drug dealers threatened to kidnap and rape his thirteen-year-old daughter. They even knew her name and which school she attended."

Karen raised a brow. "If that isn't a way to gain compliance, then I don't know what is. Absolute scum."

One of the desk phones rang as Karen was about to issue a few more instructions. An officer answered and listened quietly, before waving in Karen's direction. The look of concern on the officer's face caught everyone's attention. Jotting a few notes down, the officer thanked the person at the other end of the line and hung up.

"Karen, that was the control room. You're needed to attend a suspicious death. Officers are there at the moment. An elderly man has been discovered on the floor of his bedroom. Early indications are his wife strangled him."

Karen and her team cut short the meeting, several of them in tow behind Karen as they headed to the scene.

## 14

FIFTEEN MINUTES after control passed on the information, Karen arrived at the location. Jade and Ed shared a car with her, while Belinda and Ty followed in another. The wheels of the investigation were in full swing, with other police vehicles, a scientific services van, and Izzy's car already there. Karen took a moment to observe the road. A pleasant enough street with semi-detached houses on either side. Tall hedges which looked well-maintained shielded many of the front gardens. Neighbours gathered on the pavement opposite the house containing the crime scene.

Karen stopped by an ambulance parked outside the property. As she peered in through the side door, she saw an elderly lady lying on the bed with paramedics attending to her and a uniformed police officer hovering in the background.

The lady tussled with ambulance staff trying to lay a blanket over her. "Are we going on holiday? Is that why you're all here? What time is breakfast?"

"We're ambulance paramedics, love," an officer said, crouching down beside the woman. "You've had a bit of a shock. We just need to check you over and keep you warm."

"Is it hot where we're going? Is my husband coming? He flies planes you know," the lady said.

Karen raised a brow towards the police officer in the ambulance, who shrugged in response. "Right, let's see what this is all about," Karen said, making her way towards the house. A uniformed officer had already set up an outer cordon with police tape stretching across the front drive. Karen pulled out her warrant card and held it up in his direction. He nodded in return. "Ma'am," he replied.

Karen and the rest of her team signed in on the scene log before ducking under the tape and making their way to the front door of the property. Another officer remained on duty, keeping a close eye on who came and went. He shifted to one side as Karen approached.

"What have we got?" she asked.

"Ma'am, the occupants of the property are David and Mary Cooper. David Cooper, aged seventy-three, was found dead on his bedroom floor an hour ago," he said while checking his notes. "His wife, seventy-one-year-old Mary, was still sitting on the bed when we arrived. She's the one in the ambulance. It was a bit of a strange scene, to be honest."

"How so?" Karen asked.

"Precious and Gloria are carers who visit Mary three times a day. They are in the front lounge and both shocked and devastated. They couldn't gain access to the property this morning when no one answered the door. They used their spare key to enter and when they didn't find anyone downstairs, they made their way upstairs to discover David's body in the bedroom, face down. His wife was sitting on the bed and acting as if nothing had happened. From what we can gather from the carers, Mary has dementia, so we were finding it difficult to make any sense of what she was saying. She kept referring to Stephen. Then she changed it to Patrick. I don't know who either of those individuals are."

"Okay, thanks." Karen grabbed a pair of gloves and booties from the box beside the front door before making her way in. She turned to Jade and asked, "Can you and Ty have a chat with the carers?"

Jade nodded as she fitted the booties on to her shoes. Karen took the steps to the upstairs landing. It felt a bit congested as Karen hovered inside the doorway. A crime scene investigator knelt beside the body taking photographs of David Cooper. The victim was lying face down with one arm tucked beneath his body and a ligature wrapped round his neck.

Another officer stood close by and acknowledged Karen. "We're not getting much sense from the wife, ma'am." Karen nodded as she stepped into the bedroom and round the body. She glanced at David Cooper's face. His eyes were fixed open, his lips slightly parted. And from the hand she could see, she saw what looked like pink markings.

"Karen," came a voice from behind her.

Karen turned to see Izzy in the doorway.

"I was downstairs writing up my notes. It was getting too cramped up here, and I needed space to think."

"First impressions?" Karen asked.

"First impressions are death by strangulation," Izzy said in a hushed tone. "We've left the body in situ while SOCO does their work. It appears to be her dressing gown cord round his neck. I'll have a definite answer tomorrow when I do the post-mortem."

"A rough idea of when he died?" Karen said.

"Between six and twelve hours ago, which fits in with the time frame of when the carers left here at nine p.m."

"Okay, Izzy. Thanks for that."

Once seated comfortably in the waiting ambulance, Karen arranged for one of the forensic officers to take nail scrapings and bag up the lipstick Mary held. Though they needed to secure Mary's gown and nightie for forensic analysis, the woman's unpredictable behaviour meant they would have to wait. Mary was making things difficult by arguing with them and trying to snatch things back. For Mary's safety, Karen arranged for social services to get involved because she needed to understand Mary's state of mind and whether she was fit to be interviewed.

While officers reached out to social services, Karen took a moment to wander round the house. The state of each room reminded her of Michael Armstrong's house. Every room had been turned over, with drawers and cupboards open and the content scattered across the floor. Someone had slashed the sofa cushions and thrown the hollow fibre contents everywhere. Mattresses in each bedroom had been flipped on to their sides and empty shoeboxes lay strewn in piles.

The scene made little sense. With no sign of forced entry, and Precious and Gloria having to use their spare keys, what had taken place here?

## 15

AFTER STEPPING OUT, Jade and Ed joined Karen in the front garden. "It's a mess inside."

"Do you think she killed him?" Jade asked.

"I don't know. There was no sign of forced entry. The only other person in the house with him was his wife. The question is, was she involved in any way? Going from her state of health, unlikely," Karen replied.

"She was playing a good game of tug of war with one officer upstairs when he tried to move her. She is not weak by any means and could have snapped, attacking her husband, but because of her dementia has no recollection of it," Ed added, throwing a thumb over his shoulder back towards the house.

"That's possible, Ed. I would have expected her to use something like a photo frame or a book. To take her own dressing gown cord off and then approach her husband from behind before wrapping it round his neck and strangling him seems far-fetched. Don't you think? And it doesn't explain the house being turned over," Karen asked.

Jade and Ed both shrugged, unsure of what to say.

Karen continued. "They turned the house over in much the same way as Michael Armstrong's house was. I'm not suggesting they're connected, but two houses turned over in the same way on our patch in a matter of days feels sus to me. Both were elderly gentlemen. Did they mix in the same circles? Did they know each other?"

Ed flipped open his notepad. "When we spoke to Precious and Gloria, they both mentioned David used to argue with them. They thought he was a very difficult and aggressive man."

"What did he argue about?" Karen asked.

"Lots of different things. He would have a go at them for not looking after his wife properly. Not staying long enough to give him a break. He said he couldn't cope with her outbursts and difficult behaviour. Nothing good," Ed added. "Gloria mentioned a few weeks ago that he wanted to get rid of Mary and ship her off to a care home."

"Did Mary overhear that?"

"According to Gloria, they were in the same room as Mary when he mentioned it."

"Whether Mary understood depends on how advanced her dementia is. If she understood, then with her state of mind she could have snapped. But I don't think it's that. Can you ask Ty and Belinda to rally a few officers to help them do door-to-door enquiries?"

"What if residents ask what happened? We can't hide the fact there is a black mortuary van outside the Coopers' house," Ed said.

Karen scrunched her nose as she looked over her shoulder to where residents had congregated to watch the comings and goings. "If anyone asks, David Cooper passed away in suspicious circumstances and we have begun an investigation. That's it. We need to ask residents if they heard or saw anything before nine p.m."

Jade stayed with Karen while Ed headed off to grab Belinda and Ty to begin house-to-house enquiries. "It's a quiet, nice little street," Jade said, blowing out her cheeks. "It will come as quite a shock to the neighbours."

"Yep. We'll do our best to deal with their concerns over safety. At least there'll be a police presence here for the next day or so while SOCO do their fingertip search of the property. Cases like this can really rock a neighbourhood and can be frightening for elderly residents. We might need to play it down a bit and assure them it's an isolated incident."

"That will be a hard one to sell, Karen. Especially when they hear about the other elderly victim."

The officer monitoring the doorway beckoned Karen over. "You're needed upstairs, ma'am."

Karen stepped through the doorway and padded up the stairs again, stopping to look at the photos pinned to the wall. A few showed David and Mary Cooper sitting round a table with five other people of a similar age to them enjoying a night out at a restaurant, all their glasses raised in toast. David and Mary looked younger, perhaps in their forties, and in happier times. Karen climbed the last few steps to find a crime scene investigator standing on the landing waiting for her.

The investigator pulled down her mask and offered Karen a small smile. "Ma'am, we've turned the body over and discovered something which might interest you. Have a look."

Karen followed the investigator back into the bedroom. It was her first opportunity to see David Cooper's face. There was extensive bruising to his cheekbone, dried blood beneath his nose, and a swollen eye.

The CSI knelt beside the body and pointed to Cooper's right hand and a fresh wound. "They have cut his right little finger off." The investigator picked up a small clear evidence bag from beside the body and held it up for Karen to see. Inside was the missing digit.

The development shocked and concerned Karen. In her opinion, it was unlikely Mary had murdered her husband, though whether she could offer a valuable insight into what she'd witnessed was another matter altogether. Two elderly men had been strangled in less than a week. A digit had been removed from both of their right hands. Their houses had been turned over. She was certain the same perpetrator was responsible for both murders and, whatever the motive, was looking for something he believed they had in their possession.

## 16

WHILE HER TEAM members were still knocking on doors and searching for any doorbell or CCTV footage that could assist their investigation, Karen took a break and strolled round the back garden of the Coopers' property, where no one could disturb her. There was a hive of activity out front with an increasing presence of neighbours, bystanders, and the curious. Karen drafted in extra PCSOs to keep the crowd at a distance. A local press team had arrived and was sniffing round for juicy titbits by taking soundbites from neighbours. It wouldn't be long before details were in every local newspaper, online news websites, and dozens of Instagram and TikTok live feeds.

It saddened her that people who passed away under suspicious circumstances were not given privacy or respect. Social media came with many advantages and just as many disadvantages. Karen had lost count of the number of times she had relied on social media to help gather information and evidence to speed up enquiries. It was a godsend because every aspect of human life was there for everyone to see. She had led many investigations where a suspect had tripped themselves up by providing an alibi, only to be caught out by evidence to the contrary on their social media platforms.

The Coopers' house could appear on mobile phones round the globe in a few seconds, with hundreds if not thousands of comments appearing, with some being both cruel and hurtful to the family.

Karen paused at the rear of the garden and looked back at the house. It did not differ from the houses on either side. Clean and well maintained. The Coopers' garden needed a good tidy-up. The grass was a little overgrown. Weeds flourished in the flower beds and dying flowers needed to be cut back. She imagined David had never found the time to venture out here, and yet this was their home, and a place where they could see out the rest of their years.

As she made her way back to the house, Karen noticed the first autumn rains had created a soft and spongy texture on the grass.

The officer on the door was talking to a man wearing jeans and a grey hoodie, with a courier bag draped across his shoulder. On seeing Karen marching through the hallway, the officer stepped to one side to catch her attention. "Ma'am, this is Grant Chilvers, a social welfare officer who's been looking after the Coopers."

Karen put Grant in his early thirties, fresh-faced, unshaven but smiley, and excitable. Karen shook his hand before inviting him in and through to the front lounge. They had released Precious and Gloria after the carers gave their statements, so Karen had the room to herself. She took a seat on one sofa and Grant grabbed the armchair.

"Thanks for coming over. I'm Detective Chief Inspector Karen Heath, the SIO on the case. We'd like to interview Mary Cooper, but we are unsure how to proceed because of her dementia. We believe she may have witnessed the attack on her husband. As you can imagine, her insights might be invaluable."

Grant nodded and offered Karen a sympathetic smile. "It's a tough one. Dementia affects everyone in different ways. In Mary's case, she struggles to remember recent events. If you asked her what she had for breakfast this morning, she won't remember. She also finds it hard to follow conversations and forgets the names of friends and everyday objects round her. If you held up a hairbrush in front of her and ask her what it was, Mary would stare at it and not say anything."

As she listened to Grant continue to describe Mary's condition, which included her feeling anxious, angry, and regularly losing the thread of what she was saying, and struggling to recall things she's heard, seen, or read, it wasn't the news Karen wanted to hear.

"It's not looking encouraging then?" Karen grimaced.

"I'm afraid not," Grant replied. "Her condition will cause mood swings and physical outbursts. In a few cases, sufferers experience hallucinations and delusions."

Karen tipped her head back and sighed. "We have to talk to her. Will you accompany me?"

Grant nodded and followed Karen to the ambulance, where Mary sat slumped on the bed, her head bobbing with tiredness.

Crouching beside Mary's chair, Grant softly placed a hand on her arm. "Mary, it's Grant. How are you doing? Do you remember me?"

Mary's eyes flickered before looking towards Grant. It took a few moments for her to reorientate herself back into the bedroom. "Stephen, what are you doing here? Would you like a cup of tea?"

"Who's Stephen?" Karen whispered.

Grant shrugged and mouthed, "No idea". He nodded for Karen to chip in.

"Mary, I'm Karen, a police officer. Do you know what's happened?"

Mary turned to Karen. "Happened? Yes. David. He's on the floor."

The lucid response took Karen and Grant by surprise, both exchanging a glance.

"Do you know what happened to him?" Karen asked.

"Happened? Did I do that?"

"We want to know what happened to David, your husband. Did you see anything? Did someone come into the bedroom?"

Mary stared at Karen, her expression flat and unresponsive. "Who hurt my David? He's a good man. Worked ever so hard."

"That's what we're trying to find out," Karen said. "Who hurt David?"

"Who's David? I don't know anyone called David."

Karen's shoulders slumped. They'd lost the moment in a blink of an eye. She sighed and stared at Grant, who looked as dejected.

Karen's phone buzzed in her jacket pocket, and she was about to retrieve it when Mary blurted out, "Money."

Karen's eyes widened. "What was that Mary? Money? What about money?"

Mary looked at Grant and then at Karen. "Do you remember the holiday we went on?"

Karen stood, her knees cracking. She grabbed her phone and read the text message on the screen.

Kelly: *Get back to the station ASAP!*

*Shit. Now what?*

"Grant, something has come up and I'm needed back at the station right away. Can we talk about Mary when I get a moment later?"

"Sure," he replied, not taking his eyes off Mary as he stroked the back of her hand. "I'll arrange for Mary to be taken to safer accommodation. I'll text you the address."

## 17

Karen tucked her bag beneath her desk and threw off her jacket, looping it over the back of the chair before heading upstairs to see her boss. Random events like this unnerved her. There was no warning or heads-up before Kelly's message, which worried Karen as she turned off the stairwell and slipped in through the door. The corridor was silent, with doors either side closed, but with glass-panelled walls she saw most of the senior officers were on the phone or in meetings.

Kelly's door was open as she approached and as she turned into the doorway and knocked. Another man sat across the desk from Kelly, both silent and staring at her. She recognised him straight away from the management structure she had studied of the North Yorkshire police force. Her muscles twitched and her heart quickened as she felt the first fluttering in her stomach.

"Karen, come in and take a seat. Close the door behind you." Kelly's tone was serious as she studied Karen.

"Yes, ma'am."

"Karen, I'd like you to meet ACC Damien Jackson from HQ."

Karen cleared her throat and extended a hand in his direction. "Sir."

Jackson nodded and shook Karen's hand, but remained silent.

Karen eased herself into a seat beside the ACC, a sense of awkwardness filling the room as Karen fought to control her breathing and composure as every worst-case scenario flashed through her mind. *Did I speak out of turn with someone? Did I miss a piece of crucial information in an earlier case? Is anyone hurt?* She had toed the line in York more than she had ever done in London. Her eyes darted back and forth between Jackson and Kelly.

"Is everything okay?" Karen asked, the pitch of her voice rising as nerves got the better of her. She tucked her clammy hands into her lap, keen to hide her sweaty palms.

Kelly smiled for the first time. "ACC Jackson was alerted to the scene you attended this morning, and as a result, the ACC needed to come here to brief us." Kelly looked across to her superior.

Karen furrowed her brow and turned towards Jackson, staring at him with a hint of curiosity. *Perhaps I haven't done anything wrong at all?*

Jackson's tall and thin frame, along with his lack of body fat, gave him a youthful complexion with taut skin. Wearing a grey suit, white shirt, and a sky-blue tie, he looked every inch the professional businessman Karen had seen hundreds of times in the Square Mile, the heart of the financial district of London.

"DCI, Laura has told me how much she values your tenacity, depth of experience, and professionalism. We regard you as one of our most senior officers so, what I have to tell you now can go no further than you and your team. Is that understood?"

"Of course, sir," Karen replied, blinking hard and glancing towards Kelly, both pleased and flabbergasted at Kelly's feedback. Kelly offered Karen the slightest of nods but remained grave-faced.

Jackson offered a simple nod. "David Cooper was in the witness protection scheme (WPS)."

It felt like someone had shoved her, as Karen swayed at the mention of a WPS. "I wasn't expecting to hear that. There's nothing on the system."

"When he was placed in witness protection, his file was kept confidential, and only details about his circumstances were shared on a need-to-know basis with my or the CC's clearance. Laura didn't know about it either," Jackson added, throwing a look in Kelly's direction.

"You said, *was*, sir?"

Jackson nodded. "Correct. As you know, you can enter a witness protection scheme voluntarily, but Cooper didn't follow the rules and the authorities removed him from the scheme two years ago. There's only so much we can do to protect an individual, and being within a WPS allows us to offer a high level of security. However, if someone chooses not to stick to the agreement then we have no choice but to release them from the scheme and leave them to fend for themselves."

It sounded harsh, but Karen had placed witnesses in protection when she'd worked at the Met. Mostly the scheme worked well, but the death of Anne Woodland, a witness her team was transporting to court, sadly tainted her memories of the WPS. Her convoy had come under attack, which led to two police officers losing their lives and the kidnap and death of Anne. They later found her body bound and shot in the head on farmland near Chelmsford in Essex.

Jackson continued. "The house the Coopers were living in was not one of our safe houses, but we had it on our watch list for any calls into the control room linked to the address. I was informed earlier, which is why I needed to come and discuss the case with you."

"Right. I see, sir."

Jackson paused for a moment and let out a deep breath. "David and Mary Cooper are not their real names. It's William and Jean Armstrong."

Karen's eyes widened in shock as her mouth fell open. She did a double take between Jackson and Kelly as the penny dropped.

Kelly nodded as if sensing Karen's realisation.

Jackson updated Karen on the circumstances leading to William going into a WPS. "Michael Armstrong is William's older brother. We are concerned and have made the investigation a top priority because your cases are connected. I need your team to drop everything else they are doing and focus on this double murder investigation,

DCI," Jackson said, the seriousness in his tone reflecting the gravity of the situation.

"Of course, sir. It's all my team is working on."

Jackson continued to brief Karen about the circumstances of William Armstrong being placed in the scheme. Armstrong had left it because his wife's dementia had led to many awkward exchanges with neighbours at the house provided to them under the scheme. With new identities, new backgrounds, and their movements monitored, Jean Armstrong's condition led to her walking off often and being found in town in a distraught state. One minute she was telling bystanders and the police she was Jean Armstrong, and the next, she was Mary Cooper, and how they were hiding from people who wanted to kill her husband.

With her condition deteriorating and William Armstrong becoming more argumentative with those tasked with his protection, and often ignoring their instructions, they had little choice but to release the couple from the scheme.

Karen continued listening and digesting everything Jackson spoke about. It was a lot to take on board. Not only did her double murder investigation ratchet up a level, but everything her team did was now under the scrutiny of ACC Jackson.

"Do you have any questions, DCI?" Jackson finished, rising from his seat and doing up the button on his suit jacket.

"I don't think so, sir. With your permission I'll brief my team."

Jackson nodded. "Stick to the script. Only discuss with them everything Laura or I have mentioned. Keep the investigation tight. The news doesn't travel any further than the SCU and my office. I also expect a daily update. Is that okay?"

"Of course, sir. Phone or email?"

"Email. We need to do this by the book, and I need to make sure we have everything documented, including your updates."

"Understood, sir. Thank you for your time," Karen said, rising to her feet to shake Jackson's hand before he strode out of the office.

It was a few seconds before either Karen or Kelly spoke. Neither sure what to say. It was Kelly who broke the silence.

"Are you okay with that? Trust me, it knocked the shit out of me too when the ACC briefed me. This is heavy-duty stuff which puts us under the spotlight, so lean on me if there is anything you need or want to discuss, okay?" Kelly said.

"Of course, and thank you, ma'am," Karen said as she turned and left the room, her eyes wide with shock as she blew out her cheeks and strolled back to her floor while processing the conversation. She whipped out her phone and sent a text to her team on-site at the Coopers', requesting they return to the office at once. Needing space to think, Karen took a detour, darting out of the back door of her building towards the grassy banks behind her office.

# 18

AFTER ABOUT AN HOUR, Karen returned to the SCU, her head clearer, her mind focused. Jade, Ed, Bel, and Ty were deep in discussion as Karen pushed open the doors and made her way to the front. Many of her officers stopped what they were doing and looked on in confusion as Karen dropped her notepad on a desk beside the whiteboards and turned to face her team.

Karen stuffed her hands in her pockets and cast her eyes round the room. She lowered the tone of her voice to express the seriousness of the situation. "I want you all to listen to what I have to say next. I'm going to share something important with you all, and it must not leave this room. Please keep it confidential and do not share it with anyone, including your family and friends. If I find anyone who has blabbed outside of these four walls, I will remove you from my team with immediate effect, and if the ACC has anything to do with it, they will probably kick you out of the force. Do I make myself clear?"

Every single one of her officers stared at her with a mixture of disbelief and astonishment etched on their features. Other than Jade, no one in the team had heard Karen speak this way, which alarmed many of them. A few officers exchanged nervous glances. Others furrowed their brows, while a few folded their arms across their chests and sat back, hanging on Karen's every word.

"I've been to the super's office and ACC Damien Jackson was there. He informed me David Cooper used to be in a witness protection scheme for three years until being kicked out two years ago for ignoring the rules and conditions placed upon him and his wife."

A few gasps rippled round the room as the news sunk in.

"David Cooper was not his real name. It was the name given as part of his new identity. His real name is William Armstrong, the younger brother of Michael Armstrong, our first victim."

"Shit," Belinda muttered.

"Exactly." Karen nodded.

"Do we have a why?" Ty asked.

Karen turned and tapped the picture of William Armstrong on the whiteboard. After ACC Jackson had left, Kelly filled Karen in on the background to the Armstrong case. "William was one of two former accountants for Denby Construction Limited. They blackmailed him into being the money man for Paul and Lee Harman. Denby Construction was awarded contracts to build commercial buildings round the north-east after strong lobbying by Nigel Flynn, a Kent MP."

Ed tutted. "I've heard of the Harman brothers before. Paul Harman managed Denby Construction. Known to have strong criminal connections in the north-east and north-west. He's now serving a twelve-year stretch for fraud."

Karen nodded in agreement as Ed continued.

"Paul blackmailed Nigel Flynn after someone took photos of him with a rent boy in one of the seedy bars owned by a Harman associate. Needless to say, they would be enough to end his political career if he didn't comply."

"The Harman brothers had a politician in their back pocket, using his influence in political circles to smooth out any local objections to contracts being awarded to Denby Construction?" an officer asked.

"Pretty much," Ed said in reply. "Lee Harman, the younger, is the mastermind. A powerful York crime lord and businessman with assets and connections in Spain and Peru. Claims to be legit and his accounts suggest that, but he was running two sets of books. From the intelligence gathered on the Harmans' operation, Peru is a major cocaine producing region. Lee Harman is as bad as it gets. We know that his organisation is infamous for kneecapping their rivals, and we suspect that his contacts and acquaintances have committed more than a dozen drug-related killings."

Ed turned to Karen. "It might be worth you talking to one of the other teams who've investigated the Harmans. It's not an exaggeration to say they are as bad as the Krays. As far as I can remember, they've amassed a fortune of over a hundred million pounds through their murders, extortion, robbery, and drug trafficking. Though not confirmed, it was alleged that they buried one of their victims in the concrete under the Etihad Stadium in Manchester."

"Okay, thanks Ed. That's really helpful. As you've heard, we are dealing with very dangerous people, which is why we need to keep this investigation as tight as possible. Please be extra cautious and vigilant with your own safety," Karen said, addressing all her officers.

Karen grabbed a marker pen and added Denby Construction to the whiteboard. "They eventually released William Armstrong from witness protection after three years when he couldn't stick to police and NCA rules. He and his wife have been in hiding for the past two years." Karen explained how Mary's dementia and increasingly erratic behaviour was causing concern to the authorities and, with William Armstrong becoming difficult to deal with, they had little choice other than to release him from the scheme.

"So William was aware of all of the Harmans' *other* activities? And that's why they were after him?" Preet asked.

Karen nodded. "It's believed William Armstrong siphoned off money to the tune of one hundred and fifty grand for his own personal gain and fixed the books to hide it. Now out of protection, we believe the Harmans tracked him down looking for the stolen money," Karen said.

"That would explain why their houses were turned over," an officer commented to no one in particular.

"And his brother, Michael? How was he involved?" Claire asked, remaining silent until now.

"We think Michael played no part in William's activities and was innocent throughout. Sadly, I think they targeted

Michael in the hope he would reveal his brother's whereabouts and he paid the ultimate price for the association."

"That's awful," Jade said, rubbing her temples. "What a nightmare. You mentioned he was one of two accountants. What happened to the other one?"

"Robert Bagshaw, age fifty-seven. We also moved him and his family into witness protection for their own safety with new identities, backstory, and a home in Kent. Unfortunately, he couldn't stick it out either and walked away. His current location is unknown. He cut all ties with the police. Bank accounts in his name were cleared out when he left. He took his daughter out of school, and there are no council tax records, phone records, or medical notes. He's gone underground. There were rumours he's taken his family abroad, but he may have returned to York as his mother is unwell."

"Was Bagshaw in cahoots with William?" Jade asked.

Karen shrugged. "We are not sure. The Super said that, in police interviews conducted at the time, he claimed to know nothing about the Harmans' criminal activities. It appears they employed Bagshaw to manage the legit books, so his defence is plausible. He may have been aware of William's activities, whether he was part of it is a different matter." Karen continued by providing further details that ACC Jackson had shared with her.

"Where does it leave the investigation?" Belinda asked.

"If we work on the assumption that the Harmans are trying to track down the missing money, we have to turn our attentions to their OCG. Start pulling up everything we have on them and their associates. Who are their enforcers? Who would they use to attack, torture, or kill their victims?

Paul is in prison and Lee wouldn't get his hands dirty. He's too clever for that. Look at all their connections."

Ty raised his pen to get Karen's attention. "What are we doing about Jean Armstrong then? It's unlikely she was involved in her husband's death in the light of what we've just heard. As far as we know she saw her husband being tortured and murdered."

"The welfare team have moved Jean to secure accommodation, and I'll visit her tomorrow morning. I'll need to assign officers on protection detail for her. In the meantime, can we run a search on William's financial and banking records? Unless William revealed the location of the money and gave his killer the details, it will be stashed somewhere. We need to locate it."

# 19

THE COUNCIL'S welfare team provided secure accommodation for Jean Armstrong, before a planned move to a hotel room with police protection. However, Grant Chilvers had convinced Karen that Jean would receive better care with trained dementia care nurses on-site twenty-four-seven, which would be difficult to offer in a hotel. He'd also highlighted how a new environment could cause anxiety, stress, and fear among dementia sufferers because it took them away from a familiar setting. Two new locations within twenty-four hours wouldn't be helpful for Jean's condition.

Though Karen wasn't comfortable with the idea to begin with, Grant's reasoning made sense to her in the end, so she'd arranged for police protection to be switched to the secure accommodation.

As Karen sat with Jean today to ask more questions, the woman was no better and provided no new information. She'd hoped Jean could provide an insight into the man who had attacked and killed her husband, but her questions were met with vague responses and statements without direct links to what Karen was asking. Karen felt sorry for the woman. Over her career in London, she had come across victims and family members with various forms of dementia while tackling cases. In each case, the sufferer was often confused, scared, made little sense, and displayed erratic behaviour. Jean was no different. Karen couldn't imagine what Jean was feeling, but she imagined it was some if not all of the things she had seen in other sufferers.

On two occasions Jean had asked after William, and though Grant and Karen had tried to explain the situation to her, they'd both doubted if she fully understood. There was one particular phrase which had piqued Karen's interest. Jean had blurted out, "he shouldn't have done that." However, when Karen had pushed, Jean hadn't been able to elaborate further, which frustrated Karen. *Is she referring to her husband or the killer?*

---

HAVING COME straight from the secure accommodation, Karen waited for Jade outside the mortuary at York Hospital.

This part of the hospital saw less traffic simply because it contained only the mortuary and linen stores. The semi-darkness and sombre atmosphere in the corridor matched Karen's mood as she scrolled through her emails. The odd porter passed her, wheeling a trolley with dirty linen towards a storeroom. Karen smiled each time to lighten her mood more than anything else, but each porter seemed to appreciate the sentiment.

Karen was away with the fairies when Jade jabbed her with a finger, making her jump. "Jesus, stop creeping up on me like that."

Jade laughed. "Gotcha." Jade glanced up and down the corridor. Quiet, gloomy, and creepy. "Here is a question for you: why are mortuaries always in the bowels of a hospital and away from civilisation? It's like they're preparing you for what's beyond these doors," she said, nodding towards the entrance.

"Jade, you come up with the most hilarious observations. They are hardly going to put the mortuary next to the café, or beside the maternity unit, or a children's ward, let alone a geriatrics ward! Can you imagine?" Karen laughed.

Jade joined her. "Talking of old people, that reminds me. Old people at weddings always poke me in the arm and say, "You're next, lovely." So, I've started doing the same thing to them at funerals." Jade chuckled to herself, amused at her own dark humour.

"Oh my God, Jade. Stop it. You're terrible," Karen replied, pressing the buzzer on the door.

They were shown into the examination room where the post-mortem on William Armstrong was in its final stages. A member of Karen's team had attended as the police representative from the beginning, so they hadn't missed anything. Karen and Jade took over, allowing the other officer to head back to the office.

"Probably a formality, but is there anything interesting to report?" Karen asked.

Izzy stepped back and examined the remains of the cadaver. She blew out a breath which puffed up her face mask.

"Nothing major. William was in good health. There were fibrosis on his lungs and most of his organs were of average weight and condition for someone of his age."

Karen moved in closer and examined William's body. His skin was pale and saggy where he had lost muscle tissue in later life, which meant his bony skeleton left his joints looking gnarly and fragile. The bruising was very clear round his neck.

"The cause of death was strangulation. He has a fracture to his cheekbone and an eye socket. There's soft tissue damage to the surrounding area consistent with receiving a blow to the face. Here is another interesting thing," Izzy said, picking up the right hand. "Stating the obvious, they cut his last digit off, and the bone stub matches the pattern on the digit found on the floor. But that's not it." Izzy pointed to the index finger and wiggled it in a circle.

Karen and Jade grimaced as they watched the finger move in a complete three-hundred-and-sixty-degree circle and bend in ways it shouldn't as if made of rubber.

"He suffered a fresh break on his finger, and it's likely it occurred right before his death."

Karen looked across at Jade before she turned her attention to Izzy. "They tortured him in the hope he would reveal where the money was. The poor bloke."

Izzy stepped away from the table and pulled her face mask down to her chin before blowing out her cheeks. "It looks that way. Beaten, tortured, and then strangled."

Karen thanked Izzy for her time before they left.

## 20

IN NEED of a break and refreshments before returning to the office, Karen and Jade headed to Crumbs Cupcakery, a pretty little tea room and bakery a few of her local officers had raved about. It had been on Karen's bucket list of places to visit for a few weeks but she'd never found the time.

As she stepped through the doors, glorious and sweet baking aromas smothered her. Owned by twin sisters who baked on-site, visitors could enjoy a cup of tea and handmade cupcakes while watching the owners busily baking more wonderful creations. It was the cosy and warm, inviting atmosphere which appealed to Karen. Pictureless gold frames hung from the walls, bunting hung from the beamed ceiling and the small dining tables with multicoloured chairs reminded Karen of colourful furniture from the sixties. It was small and quaint, but perfect and personal.

"Oh my God, I think I've put on a stone in weight just looking at these gorgeous creations," Jade squealed, her eyes fixed wide as she scanned the choice. "Victoria 99. Salted caramel. Snickers. Raspberry Bakewell. I think I've died and gone to heaven."

"That's what a lot of our customers say," Charlotte, the owner, said as she appeared from the rear of the bakery.

Karen stood beside Jade. "Oh, Jesus, I'm going to have to loosen the button on my trousers. No wonder everyone has been raving about this place. My shout, have what you want, and then I'll take back a few boxes to treat the team. You've got an amazing selection here. I'd be eating all the profits if I worked here," Karen sighed, rubbing her belly.

"I won't lie, me and Jen are forever sampling our cupcakes… for quality control, of course!"

"Of course," Karen replied as she rolled her eyes.

Karen ordered the salted caramel and Jade chose the raspberry white chocolate along with a coffee each before grabbing a table away from a few customers.

"What a cute little place. A real hidden gem," Jade remarked, taking in the decor.

They tucked into the cupcakes, ooohs, and aaahs tripping from their tongues every few seconds.

Jade leaned across the table and kept her voice down. "Do you think the killer has found the money?"

Karen dabbed her lips with a tissue and shrugged. "I don't know. It's uncertain if anything was taken. The killer was looking for anything which would lead him to the money." Karen sidetracked for a moment. "Their ruthlessness terrified Armstrong. They found Nigel Flynn, MP, dead beside a rent boy. Both had plastic bags taped round the heads, and their wrists tied to the bedpost. The police carried out an investigation, and this wasn't some sick sex game which had gone wrong. According to the ACC, Flynn was about to go to the police because he was being blackmailed. It's believed the Harman brothers needed to shut him up, permanently."

Jade listened intently as she sipped her coffee, enjoying the contrast between its bitterness and the sweetness of the cupcakes.

"William Armstrong couldn't handle it any more and left. According to him, Paul Harman threatened to bury him and his wife Jean alive in coffins deep in the woods to suffer a slow and painful death."

Jade bared her teeth. "Christ."

"Anyway, Armstrong went to the police, and then the shit hit the fan. Denby Construction came under investigation for tax fraud, and they took Paul and his company to court. They sent him down on Armstrong's confession, which also included pointing police to crucial evidence, but only if we protected him from retribution. Armstrong went into witness protection and then continued to give his evidence."

"A man with a target on his back," Jade remarked.

"How are you getting on?" Charlotte said, approaching the table. "Is there anything else I can get you?"

Karen nodded. "Can you make up a few random boxes for me? Twenty-four cupcakes?"

"Of course I can. Thank you. I'll have those ready for you before you leave."

Karen thanked Charlotte and waited for her to leave before continuing.

"Based on Armstrong's evidence, the investigating team executed twelve search warrants and found a hidden ledger, which Armstrong had mentioned being hidden at one property. When they examined the books, they noted a monthly turnover of three hundred and twenty thousand pounds, which exceeded what they'd declared in the official accounts." Karen wrapped official in air quotes.

"So Armstrong was the money man who knew all their dirty secrets?" Jade said.

Karen nodded. "Yep. As part of the operation, the team also recovered over seventy thousand pounds in cash, thirty thousand pounds of which were hidden in a modified vehicle. The Harmans are clever bastards. As the investigation delved deeper, it exposed additional details, including the unearthing of another ledger in a confiscated car. The ledger showed the Harmans had sold drugs worth over £1.8 million over thirty-five months."

Jade sat back in her chair, her eyes wide in shock. "How does the reference to the missing money fit into all of this?"

Karen checked over her shoulder to make sure no one had taken the table behind them before she continued. "William Armstrong siphoned off more than a hundred and fifty grand for himself as a safety net *before* going to the police. I guess he saw it as severance pay."

Jade tapped her fingers on the table. "So we need to find the money and a murderer."

"Pretty much. And I love a challenge, so if I can find the links between the murderer and the Harmans, we can bring down their OCG as well, but first I want to pay Lee Harman a visit."

Jade placed her elbows on the table and rested her face in her hands. "Don't you think we've had enough of OCGs already? The Connells were bad enough, but the Harmans sound like they are the next level up on the 'fuck, they are scary' scale."

Karen drained the last of her coffee and pushed back her chair. "Right, let's get out of here before I order another round of coffees and cupcakes. I don't think Zac would like me if I can't fit through his front door."

## 21

KAREN DROPPED Jade back at the station and left her to bask in the glory of arriving laden with calorie-busting cupcakes, while she made her way to an address close to the railway station. Hudson Quarter was a stylish and modern development of residential and commercial properties. Karen had learned that Lee Harman had both his office and luxury penthouse apartment in the same development.

Further updates posted on the system from the crime scene investigators had confirmed Michael Armstrong's house was clean, with no prints inside the door and no signs of forced entry. Somehow, the killer had talked his way into the property without concerning Michael, in much the same way he'd gained access to William Armstrong's house. Karen could only assume the killer had been in disguise and offered a plausible reason why he'd needed entry. There was no forensic evidence by the door to suggest there had been a violent struggle.

A nagging question continued to bounce round Karen's mind. Why had the killer meticulously removed the little finger from both victims? The image evoked memories of a previous case, where she'd seen similar brutal tactics.

Karen parked in the visitors' bay and made her way to the ground-floor reception. She nodded, taking in the double-height atrium and generous space with clean lines, modern and contemporary furniture, and decorative lighting which hung from long cables.

"Do you have an appointment?" the receptionist asked.

"No," Karen said, presenting her warrant card.

"I'm afraid Mr Harman won't see anyone without an appointment."

Karen rolled her eyes. "He'll see me," she said, glancing towards the open elevator door as she made a beeline for it.

"Excuse me, officer. I'm sorry but you can't go there!" the receptionist shouted, jumping up from her seat and racing round the long desk towards Karen.

Karen thanked the woman with a curt smile and stepped in, pressing the button before she could stop her. Alone in the elevator and with the shouts of the ground-floor receptionist fading, Karen glanced to her left and gave herself the once-over in the gleaming mirrors surrounding her. Quicker than she imagined, the elevator chimed, and the doors opened. A smart woman in a grey two-piece suit and white blouse, with her hair pinned back into a stylish ponytail placed her phone down and raced towards Karen.

"I'm sorry, but you're not allowed up here without an appointment."

Karen looked at the woman. Slim, strikingly attractive, mid-twenties. A name badge told Karen her name was

Carly. "No, I don't have an appointment. It's a very last-minute thing," Karen said, pulling out her warrant card and presenting it to Carly. "I'm dealing with a double homicide case at the moment, and I would like to talk to your boss… now."

Carly put on a fake smile as her eyes glanced at Karen's identity. "Mr Harman doesn't see people without an appointment," she said with a curtness in her tone.

"I thought you would say that. We can do this nicely, or I can come back with a team of officers and make a hell of a racket and I think all of this is above your pay grade. So I would suggest you have a word with Mr Harman and tell him I would like five minutes of his time," Karen said, throwing the woman a sarcastic smile as she folded her arms across her chest in defiance.

Carly shifted on the spot as if deciding her best course of action before she scurried off and disappeared down the corridor.

Karen rolled her eyes as she walked round, admiring the modernistic styling of the building. It was a few moments before Carly reappeared, the smile wiped from her face.

"Mr Harman has a five-minute gap in his diary and can see you. Please follow me."

Karen followed the woman down the corridor, her feet sinking into the deep pile carpet which silenced her approach. As she turned the corner, she noticed two burly men in suits standing outside a closed door. One had what appeared to be a handheld metal detector clasped between his hands. Carly stopped beside the men, offering them a discreet nod before turning and heading back towards her reception desk.

"One moment, miss. Everyone needs to be checked before seeing Mr Harman. I need to scan you, and my colleague needs to check your bag," one man said, his frame almost the size of a single doorway, with his neck so short it looked as if his head sat on his shoulders.

Karen took a step back and glared at the man, her eyes unflinching. "I'm a police officer. You have no authority to search my bag. Use your scanner, but that's as far as you go."

*No Neck*, as Karen had mentally dubbed the man, glanced at his colleague, neither of them sure what to do. His colleague was slim and tall, with cropped hair and a stubbly goatee. His eyes were deadpan as he nodded at *No Neck*.

It took a few moments to scan her before *Goatee* opened the door and allowed Karen to pass through. He closed the door behind her.

Karen glanced over her shoulder before she turned her attention towards Harman's vast and sprawling office. A large and plush white leather sofa formed a horseshoe shape at one end, while at the other, a solitary desk took a prime position by the floor-to-ceiling windows. Other than that, there was nothing in the room apart from a few doors which led to smaller glass-fronted meeting rooms. *Overkill*, Karen thought.

Karen swallowed hard as she made the short walk towards Harman's desk. Her heels clipped on the hard tiled floor, the noise echoing round the space. It felt like she was going for an interview as the nerves jangled in her belly.

Lee Harman sat with his back to her, looking through his window to the city of York beyond. He swivelled in his chair but didn't rise as Karen approached.

Though Karen had seen a few images of Lee and his brother Paul, the man looked a lot scarier in real life. His slim, weathered face seemed etched by time and brutality. Eyes as frigid as a polar ice cap drilled into her with an unsettling intensity. Dressed in an open-neck Oxford shirt and cream chinos, he would have fitted in as a city banker in Canary Wharf in London. Though she couldn't see what shoes he had on, she imagined they were suede brown brogues.

"Lee Harman?" Karen asked.

Lee leaned back in his chair and studied Karen for a few seconds. "You bloody know I am, otherwise, you wouldn't be here. So, cut the bollocks. What can I do for you?" he said, his voice flat, cold and menacing.

"I'm Detective Chief Inspector Heath from York police. I'm the senior investigating officer overseeing a case involving a double homicide. One victim was William Armstrong, a former employee of yours. The other was his brother."

Lee looked towards the ceiling and narrowed his eyes as if trying to place the name. "Doesn't mean much to me. Why are you here?" he asked.

Karen smiled and nodded once more. "That's fine. If you want to play the dumb idiot, then it works for me. William Armstrong was your accountant. You and I both know that. He was an integral part of Denby Construction, a business your brother Paul ran until his naughtiness caught up with him. William managed their accounts, and from what I can gather, money went missing. Someone associated with you, or your brother, possibly tortured the Armstrongs to find out about the missing money and later killed them when they came up empty."

Lee laughed. "Bloody hell, that's a good tale. What do you think I am? I'm not a dodgy criminal who sells crack on the street or anything like that. I run a legitimate business empire. Check my accounts if you haven't already. I have an extensive property portfolio both here and in Europe. I've invested in several smaller football clubs and casinos. Fuck, I'm even a part owner of a racehorse, and I fucking hate horse racing."

"Good for you. I'm sure you and Paul have enough connections to hire muscle to do your dirty work. William put Paul in prison. That's a strong enough motive for revenge, and with the missing money, I'm sure you were both pissed off."

Lee didn't move from his chair but nodded, Karen doing little to ruffle his feathers. His eyes widened as he wagged a finger in Karen's direction. "I remember now. I know who you are. You're the copper from London, the one who took on the Connells. You're formidable from what I gather and not to be messed with."

Karen pursed her lips as her body stiffened. She clenched her jaw and let out a slow breath. "It looks like my reputation precedes me. Well then, you know I'm not to be messed with. I will find out who murdered William and Michael Armstrong, and I will do my hardest to find the connection between their killer and you and your brother. That's my promise to you."

Lee shrugged. "If you're so insistent then be my guest, but you'll be wasting your time." Lee pressed the buzzer on his desk and the door behind Karen opened, *No Neck* appearing in the doorway. "The constable is leaving now. Show her out," he said with a cocky smirk.

"Thank you for your time," Karen said. She turned and took her time walking back over the tiled floor, taking one last look over her shoulder at Lee before stepping through the doorway. *No Neck* took her on a different route than the one Carly had used. It didn't bother Karen at first but surprised her when they passed a glass-fronted meeting room with seven men in suits sat round a table deep in discussion. They all stopped and watched her as she walked by, their eyes trailing her every step. Each one looked unsavoury as they glared at her. *Some of Harman's associates?*

## 22

Not used to waiting, frustration gnawed away at Cready. He also wasn't happy about not delivering for his client. Whenever tasked with a job, Cready would spend a few days finding and eliminating his target. This case, which had appeared straightforward on paper, was proving to be unexpectedly challenging. Instead of making progress, Cready found himself eliminating leads one after another, leaving him with fewer options than he had hoped.

Cready had already waited across the street for twenty minutes and, not wishing to draw attention to himself, had moved away and headed to a café. Walking along with a coffee in hand, he tried to blend in like any other bloke passing by. But it was hard for him because he stood out. Tall, muscly, and dressed in black, he cast a menacing figure wherever he went. He looked better suited to a boxing or MMA ring, and his presence was enough to cause people to part to let him through. Cready had ferocious strength and a natural talent for inflicting pain. He was the ideal thug for intimidating someone for information or taking someone's life in a matter of moments. His hands were the size of plates, each one being big enough to strangle someone with one hand or deliver a punch to send any victim crashing to the floor in a crumpled mess.

Though he plied his trade in Manchester, his connections with the biggest names in the criminal underworld meant he had taken jobs across the country in cities such as Leeds, London, Cardiff, and Glasgow. But wherever he went, the job didn't change. The instructions were to hurt someone or kill them. He had taken a lot of jobs in Glasgow as criminal gangs fought each other for territory. Each time someone was eliminated, it created a gap, and the violence intensified. That was where he came in, to remove the threat for whoever his client was at the time.

This job was peanuts in comparison, though it was taking longer than expected to complete. Taking up a new position, he waited, occasionally sipping from his coffee as he scanned up and down the street. His patience was rewarded when he spotted the man he was looking for. Cready crossed the road and trailed him, making sure he kept a safe distance between them, only moving forward and closing the gap as pedestrians on the street thinned out.

Darryl Adler turned off the road and headed down a side street, his pace quickening as he darted among the cars. Cready turned and sped up, his long legs making up the ground in a matter of seconds. Adler glanced over his shoulder to see Cready crossing the road and heading in his direction, a matter of feet away. Adler froze, his eyes wide with fear as he glanced up and down the road, deciding whether he had the pace to outrun Cready. Before he could move, Cready pounced, his massive hand encircling Adler's throat and slamming him against the wall. Adler fought for breath, desperate as the huge man's fingers tightened their grip. Amid his choking, he tried to mutter something.

Cready leaned into him, his face a few inches away from Adler's. Adler was a local run-of-the-mill criminal known for handling stolen goods, selling drugs, and shoplifting. Cready's enquiries with local criminals had flagged up Adler's name as a person of interest.

"I swear, I've got no money on me, but I can get you anything you want. Drugs, laptops, clothes, booze, you name it, I can get it," Adler squealed through ragged breaths.

"You don't know me, and it's better for you that you don't. You piss me off, and I'll run a knife across your belly and feed your fucking guts to the foxes. I need an address," Cready hissed.

Adler furrowed his brow. "An address. What do you mean?"

"I hear you've got connections in the council. I need an address for someone."

Adler tried to shake his head. "I don't know anyone in the council."

Cready tightened his grip, forcing Adler to splutter and cough as his face reddened. "That's your one lie. You give me another one and you won't see tomorrow. Get me an address, and there's five hundred quid in it for you."

The mention of money caught Adler's attention as he nodded. "What's the name?"

Cready retrieved a small piece of paper from his back pocket and handed it to Adler. "Get me his address."

Adler nodded again.

Cready held Adler against the wall but stepped back and landed a hard right fist into the man's belly. Adler screamed in pain as his body went limp. Cready let go as the man collapsed to the floor and curled up into a little ball. Glancing round, Cready spotted a woman pushing a pram on the other side of the road. She looked across at him and quickened her step as she hurried away.

"I'll get it. How can I get in touch with you?"

Cready knelt down. "I'll find you. Don't even think about doing a runner. It's an easy five hundred quid and if you lie, well… You have a girlfriend and a little baby, don't you?"

Adler shrank back even further as he whimpered.

"Elaine, right? And your baby girl is Bella." Cready nodded as Adler stared at him. "I know who they are, and I know where they live. I'll chop off both of their little fingers and leave them on the table for you as a present."

Adler gasped as he coughed.

"You have until tomorrow morning." Cready stood and walked away, leaving Adler crying.

## 23

KAREN STRODE into her office and dropped her bag beside her desk before turning and heading to the window. She curled her hands into fists and slammed them hard on the windowsill. Her visit to Lee Harman had both angered and rattled her. The spectre of the Connells hung over her wherever she went. York was supposed to have been a fresh start, but it was tainted with her experience in London. Karen realised that, no matter where her career took her, the shadows of her past clung to her like an inescapable curse. She ground her teeth as her thoughts turned towards Lee Harman. Anger prickled her skin as she thought about her meeting with him.

"Is everything okay?" Jade asked, walking into the office just as Karen slapped her hands on the windowsill again.

Karen groaned and turned before taking in a deep breath and blowing out her cheeks. "Lee bloody Harman."

Jade rolled her eyes as she dropped into the chair opposite Karen's desk. "Didn't go too well?" Jade asked, taking a sip of coffee from her mug and kicking her shoes off to make herself more comfortable.

"Lee Harman comes across as an intimidating individual, but he also has such a big ego, his head probably won't fit through most doors. I turned up at his office and not only did I get the once-over with a metal detector from one of his heavies, but his actual office was huge. He sat at one end behind a desk and there was a leather sofa at the other. Nothing in between. There was space to fit twenty desks in there," Karen said with a shrug.

"Did you get anywhere?"

Karen shook her head and sat, before running her fingers down her face and letting out a frustrated sigh. "He denied any involvement. Harman pretended to not recall William Armstrong's name. He might run a legitimate business empire, but I question how he amassed his fortune. His questionable business dealings have a well-crafted front."

Jade leaned forward, her eyes focused on Karen. "I'll get the team to pull up everything we have on Lee Harman."

"Thanks, Jade. I'm going to see Paul Harman tomorrow and I'll take Ty with me. I want to look him in the eye as well, though if he's like his brother, he'll deny all knowledge and responsibility, but that's the game we play, hey?"

"Yep," Jade replied. "The team is still going through the CCTV crawl. It threw up fresh evidence. The team found the route the car followed on the night Michael was killed. The footage is stopped by another car for a moment, and we catch another sight of the killer getting out. It's not a brilliant image because it was dark at the time. The driver wore a black jacket, dark trousers, and a black baseball cap.

We didn't get a clear image of his face, but we believe him to be dark skinned."

"Okay, not a total disaster. Was anyone else in the other car?"

"No. The suspect retrieved what looked like a jerrycan from the boot of the car before driving off again. My guess is it contained petrol which was used as an accelerant on Michael and the car. We've checked with local officers and the car isn't there now. An old, black 3 Series BMW running on stolen plates belonging to a navy 3 Series BMW. The interesting thing is the person we believe to be the killer returned about two hours later on foot and drove off in the BMW."

"That car could be anywhere now. Set up an ANPR alert for the registration and get images of the car and the suspect enhanced if you can," Karen said.

"I see the super has set up a press conference for later this afternoon. Are you taking part?"

"Yes. Another one of those last-minute things. We need to stop the press speculation, so it's better if we control the release of information. I need a coffee because I'm flagging. Any other updates?" Karen said, rising from her seat.

Jade got up and slipped her shoes back on before following Karen to the kitchen. "Bart's team completed their fingertip search of Michael Armstrong's house. They didn't find Michael's phone but found a broken SIM card beneath the dining table."

"Clever," Karen said, grabbing a mug from the cupboard and flicking on the kettle before reaching for the coffee jar.

Jade continued. "They also found birthday cards from William to Michael among the paperwork scattered round the floor. We've already run cell site analysis and reviewed phone records from his provider. There were regular calls to Michael, but when we checked the call logs from William's provider, he made no outgoing calls apart from those to Michael."

The kettle flicked off as steam poured from the spout. Karen poured boiling water into her mug and stirred it vigorously as Jade wrapped up her update. "So, William was doing his best to stay in the shadows and keep his head down. My guess is he feared the Harmans would find him one day. Though Paul is in prison, he has a powerful reach and, with Lee on the outside, the Harmans still posed a threat to his life and Jean's."

"I feel sorry for Michael. He was an innocent party in all of this but paid with his life. I wonder if he revealed William's location to his killer?" Jade said.

"Were the birthday cards from William still in their envelopes?"

"Most of them were. Why?"

"Hanging on to his birthday cards from William didn't do him any favours. They've got a postmark on them. Even if Michael didn't reveal William's exact location, the killer could at least narrow it down to a particular town or city."

Jade grimaced. "I'm done for today. Do you mind if I shoot off early? James wants to meet for dinner."

Karen and Jade walked back towards the main floor. "Not at all. You shoot off. I've got the press conference in about thirty minutes," Karen said, checking the time on her phone, "and then I'm heading off to Zac's anyway."

"Thanks, Karen. Have a good evening, and I'll see you tomorrow."

"You too," Karen said as she peeled off and headed towards her office.

## 24

THE CONFERENCE ROOM held the usual suspects from the local press and radio. Detective Superintendent Laura Kelly had been called into a meeting at the last minute, so she'd dumped Karen in it, forcing her to go solo. With just a press officer from the force sitting beside her, it felt like all eyes were on her. In a matter of a few moments, the vultures would be hanging on her every word. Karen scanned the sea of faces. Several reporters appeared to know each other as they laughed at whatever they were talking about. A few photographers lingered on the fringes of the group, making sure they had an uninterrupted view of the stage.

It wasn't long before Karen spotted her favourite pain in the arse reporter, Henry Beavis. There was something different about him on this occasion. He didn't appear his usual confident and cocky self as he stared ahead, ignoring the banter of colleagues round him. Karen stared at him for a few moments, but Henry didn't make eye contact with her once. *Odd*, she thought.

"It looks like everyone is here," the press officer whispered from behind her hand.

Karen nodded and shuffled her papers for effect, even though they had nothing to do with her case or the press briefing. "Shall we begin?" Karen said, raising her voice. All eyes turned towards her, and she felt the skin on her back prickle with heat. "Thank you for coming at short notice. York police are dealing with the double homicide of two elderly gentlemen. The first victim was Michael Armstrong, aged seventy-six, a retired pharmacist. He was a York resident for most of his life but had travelled round the country for his work. We discovered his body in his burnt-out vehicle on an industrial estate on the outskirts of the city." Karen explained the circumstances surrounding his death before moving on.

"Seventy-three-year-old David Cooper was killed at home, making him the second and most recent victim." Kelly had briefed Karen on using the name given to the victim as part of witness protection. The ACC had decided to let the press and members of the public assume the two victims were not connected until they could locate the killer.

Karen pressed a remote-control fob in her hand and the images of both victims appeared on a screen behind her. Reporters fidgeted in their chairs to get a better look, and photographers snapped away.

"The investigation is ongoing into both suspicious deaths as we gather evidence." Karen provided information about the dates, times, and locations of the deaths of Michael and David. "We are appealing to the public to come forward with information surrounding these two cases. If you were in the area and saw anything odd or suspicious, or saw someone loitering about, then we ask you to contact our hotline or Crimestoppers. Members of the public can choose to stay anonymous." Karen pressed her remote again and two numbers appeared on the screen behind her.

A reporter raised their hand in the middle of the crowd and probed Karen. "Are the two cases connected?"

"At the moment, we're trying to establish whether they had any connection."

"Were they random attacks or targeted?" the reporter pushed.

*Give me a break.*

"The nature of the attacks, the manner, and the victims' ages have led us to believe that both elderly gentlemen were targeted."

A female reporter sitting in the front row raised her hand. She had sharp angular features and piercing eyes which displayed little warmth. "As you can imagine, the elderly population always fears for their safety. They are the most vulnerable in our society and can often not defend themselves. The death of two elderly residents in such a short space of time will no doubt have alarmed many. What reassurances can you give to the elderly residents of York?"

Karen shot the press officer a brief look, who pursed her lips and offered nothing more than a small grimace in return. Karen sighed before continuing. "We believe this may have been a targeted attack, so I want to reassure our elderly residents that their safety is our paramount concern, but we do not believe there is any immediate threat to them. We are also increasing police patrols across the city as a visible reassurance." Karen spotted Henry Beavis staring at her, his face solemn. It was out of character in her opinion.

In earlier press conferences, he had been up and down in his seat like a yo-yo being a thorn in her side.

"Of course, if any elderly resident has any particular concerns about their safety, then they can reach out to us through 101, and neighbourhood officers will be visiting households and doing their utmost to reassure them and helping in whichever way they can."

Karen described sightings of a person of interest, the old black BMW he was driving, and what he looked like. Those insights spawned a flurry of questions which Karen fielded to the best of her ability without giving too much away. She stressed he was a person of interest and dangerous so must not be approached. Karen highlighted the need for members of the public to contact the police in the first instance. As everyone filtered out of the room, Karen stepped off the podium and made a beeline for Henry before he disappeared into the crowd.

"Henry, are you okay?" Karen grabbed him by the arm and pulled him to one side. "You weren't yourself in here today. You normally give me a really hard time," Karen said with a smile.

Henry looked round to make sure no one could overhear them. "I had a call while I was waiting outside to come in. Someone asking a lot of questions about you."

"Like what?" Karen asked.

"What you are like as an officer? Do you have a family? Are you always based at this nick? Did I know your shift patterns?"

Karen didn't like the sound of that. "Did you recognise the voice?"

Henry shook his head and scrunched up his nose. "It didn't sound like a social call, and he was very abrupt. There wasn't any nicety in the way he asked, and his tone sounded a bit menacing. It unnerved me a little. It worried me."

"I wouldn't worry about it, Henry. It's a hazard of the job. We get crank callers, stalkers, and threats. Can I take the number, and I'll run a search for it?"

"Sure," Henry said, pulling out his phone from his back pocket and scrolling to his call list. He read out the number for Karen, who jotted it down on her pad.

"Okay, thanks for the heads-up, Henry. I appreciate it." Karen waited as Henry sauntered back towards the main entrance. Her mind turned towards Harman. Was he behind that, knowing it might get back to her?

## 25

THE EVENING SUN had dipped beyond the horizon, but autumn warmth still lingered in the air. It felt like the perfect evening for a glass of wine on the patio and a few nibbles to melt away the stresses of the day. Karen grabbed a change of clothes from her bag and walked down the path to Zac's door. She was about to knock when the door flung open and Summer appeared, giving them both a fright. Summer jumped back and screamed, throwing a hand over her mouth as she collided with a friend behind her. Summer and her friend fell about laughing as Karen stood in the doorway grinning, though her heart pounded from the shock.

"Sorry, Karen. I didn't know you were there," Summer said.

"Ditto," Karen replied as she glanced at Summer's friend.

"Oh, Karen, this is Lottie. Lottie, this is Karen, my Dad's girlfriend."

Karen felt her cheeks flush as the heat rose up her neck. Hearing herself referred to as Zac's girlfriend felt alien to her. It was the term teens or those in their twenties would use. Or maybe she was being an old fuddy-duddy, she wasn't sure. "It's nice to meet you, Lottie. Where are you two off to?"

"We're heading into town. Just hanging around. Might meet up with friends," Summer replied, checking her phone.

"Okay, good. Be careful. Don't forget to check the charge on your phones and turn on location services. Don't talk to strangers and stay in well-lit areas. Don't lose sight of each other and stick together, understand?"

Summer giggled. "You've been spending too much time with Dad. You're beginning to sound like him."

Karen laughed. "It's only because he cares for you. Well, we both care for you. You're missing one crucial fact. Your Dad and I are both police officers, and we know *exactly* what it's like on the streets. So, we're looking out for you."

"I know, but we're not kids. And I've lost count of the number of times that Dad has drilled the importance of safety into my brain," Summer replied, jabbing her temple.

Summer had only recently turned into her teens, and she didn't see herself as a child. *How in the world did that change so quickly?*

"Well, you're still a child in the eyes of the law, whether you like it or not."

Summer and Lottie giggled again as they looked at one another. "We really have to go. Dad's inside," Summer added.

Karen stepped to one side to let the girls pass by. "Oh, how was Manky today? Has he settled in?"

Summer's eyes widened in excitement. "Oh my God, he's so gorgeous. He sleeps on my bed all day. He's so cuddly."

"That's good. He's keeping your bed warm for you, so hurry back," Karen said as she closed the door behind them and dropped her bags at the bottom of the stairs.

"Lottie seems nice," Karen shouted as she headed into the kitchen to find Zac putting dirty plates into the dishwasher. She came round his side and gave him a tender kiss on the lips. She studied her man for a few moments as her face softened. "I love you."

He closed the door on the dishwasher and wrapped his arms round her waist. "Good, because I *really* love you, too. Yes, Lottie is lovely. The only problem with the both of them is they leave the dirty plates in the sink. Pizza and garlic breadcrumbs are all over the table, and they don't push their chairs in when finished. The youth of today," Zac said, tutting before shaking his head.

Karen laughed. "Maybe you're becoming an old fuddy-duddy too."

"What does that mean?" he asked, furrowing his brow.

"Nothing. Just a conversation I had with the girls on the doorstep. Anyway, have you eaten?"

"Not yet. I was waiting for you. Do you want me to rustle something up?" he asked.

Karen scratched her nose. "No. I fancy a takeaway curry this evening and a bottle of beer. Fancy that?"

"Now you are talking. I'm up for that," he said, heading to the drawer at the far end of the counter which had all his takeaway menus.

After forty-five minutes, foil containers filled with vegetable samosas, a chicken biryani, garlic naan, roti, paneer kebabs, chilli lamb, and spicy prawns surrounded them. The aroma of aromatic spices filled the kitchen as they eyed the wonderful feast.

"Do you think we ordered a bit too much?" Karen laughed.

"It would be rude not to. That's half the fun of ordering an Indian, isn't it?" Zac replied. "There's enough for Summer if she's hungry when she gets in."

They picked through the food, savouring every mouthful as the heat and spices tickled the insides of their mouths. Zac's forehead itched as the heat from the chilli lamb left a sheen of sweat on his face. He downed half a bottle of beer to quench the raging fire which scorched his throat and belly.

"Shit, that's hot. But bloody good," he laughed.

They caught up on each other's days between each mouthful. Zac's team was hunting for a group of armed robbers who had raided three mini supermarkets in as many weeks. Karen touched on her visit to Lee Harman, with Zac offering her a friendly warning to be on her guard as he wasn't a man to be messed with.

Karen appreciated the heads-up. The call Henry had received still played on her mind. Could it have been one of Lee's associates? Did she now have a target on her back? She wanted to tell Zac about the call but didn't want to alarm him, so kept it to herself.

They tidied away and then retired to the lounge, where they dropped into the sofas and rubbed their sore and swollen bellies. Karen took a sip from her beer, the alcohol doing its job of relaxing her. She smiled to herself as she recalled seeing an old 1970s Heineken ad on YouTube and the slogan, "Refreshing the parts other beers cannot reach." Her bottle wasn't Heineken. It was Sol, but it had the same effect as her body moulded into Zac's.

"Maltesers?" Zac asked, reaching over to the coffee table to grab the sharing bag he had bought.

"Maltesers and a bottle of beer. Interesting combination!" Karen laughed. "Oh, go on. Just a few. Any more and my belly might explode."

Karen felt relaxed and contented as she snuggled into Zac. A takeaway, a few bottles of beer, a bag of chocolates, and a cuddle with her man. Simple pleasures, which now meant the world to her. She could never have imagined this scene a year or two ago. Though she had dreamt of being in a secure and loving relationship where she loved and laughed, the possibility of it becoming reality one day had never been something she had entertained. In that moment, Karen found comfort in the little things that had become the anchor of her life.

## 26

HMP LEEDS WASN'T a prison Karen had visited much during her police career. This would be her third, she recalled. After travelling an hour with Ty, they entered the visitors' block through a separate entrance to the family and relatives. She doubted they would get a warm reception if those round her knew she was a police officer. After the security personnel scanned and checked their possessions, Karen and Ty were made to wait in a separate area until an interview room was prepared.

"It looks like it's seen better days," Ty said, staring at the peeling paint on the ceiling.

"Frankly, it's a shithole," Karen replied. "A Victorian prison designed to house only six hundred prisoners has more than double that. Sanitation is awful. I visited a cell years ago and it stunk to high heaven. I swear I nearly gagged. They've found cockroaches in the kitchen stores, and the Inspectorate has slated it."

"Do the crime and do the time," Ty said. "I don't have any sympathy for them."

"Me neither. Prisons are too lenient with their populations. I've seen cells with TVs, kettles, *PlayStations,* and prisoners walking round wearing designer clothes and trainers. They're like bloody hotels. Mind you, Leeds has one of the highest death rates among prison populations. It's like a tinderbox."

A female prison officer approached them. Young, in her mid to late twenties, blonde hair tied in a ponytail. She flashed a larger-than-life smile in Ty's direction before looking at Karen. "Your interview room is ready for you, and we have escorted the prisoner there. Would you like to come with me?" she said, before turning away from Karen and smiling again at Ty, who flashed her one of his toothy grins.

Karen held in a laugh as Ty shrugged.

"What can I say? She finds me attractive," Ty said as he set off after the prison officer, with Karen following behind.

They entered an interview room and noticed that it needed repair, much like the waiting area. The lino floor had worn out, and the cream paint on the brick walls had blistered and peeled in places. The overhead fluorescent tube cast a dull glow, which washed any further colour from the room. A small camera hung from the ceiling, watching her every move as Karen entered.

Paul Harman wasn't what she had expected. He was twice the size of his brother but not in a good way. Edging closer to twenty stone, with a round face that resembled the size of a football, and fat chubby arms which strained the seams on a T-shirt which didn't reach the waistband of his joggers.

He studied both officers as they took a seat opposite him, and after a few moments, his eyes fixed on Ty, gazing at him.

"Paul Harman, I'm Detective Chief Inspector Heath from York police. This is my colleague, Detective Constable Owen."

Harman didn't look at Karen while she addressed him. His eyes remained glued in Ty's direction. "They threw you a banana and let you out of the zoo?" he snarled.

Karen glanced across to Ty, who remained impassive, not rising to the racial taunts. Prisoners went to great lengths to taunt police officers during their visits. She had lost count of the number of sexual innuendos she had received during her visits. Some were so graphic and horrific that Karen had to try her hardest to avoid being unsettled by them. It was all part of a prisoner's attempt to gain the upper hand, though in reality their bark was often worse than their bite.

Ty replied with a smile. "Mr Harman, I have my freedom and you don't. As soon as this interview finishes, I can leave and go across the road to Starbucks to enjoy a nice caramel latte and a cookie. You go back to your pokey little cell and drink your own piss."

Karen spotted a tremor in Harman's eyelids as he bristled with anger. She tried her hardest to avoid the smirk threatening to spread across her face. *Well done, Ty.*

"Mr Harman, I'm the senior investigating officer on a case involving the murder of William Armstrong, your former accountant, and his brother, Michael Armstrong. Both were strangled and had a digit cut off from one of their hands. I'm sure you've heard about it?"

Harman smirked. "Good news travels fast. Did you drive all this way to break the news to me, or were you planning to give me a hand job under the table?" Harman winked. "You'll be fine. The screws turn a blind eye to that kind of stuff."

*God, he's a piece of work.*

Karen pursed her lips and tipped her head from side to side as if considering her options. "I did think about it, but I've left my magnifying glass back at the office and without it, I'd probably have a hard time finding it!"

Harman glared at her. "Fucking sarky bitch."

Karen threw back a smile before continuing. "I'm narrowing down the motives for torturing and murdering two men in their seventies in their homes," Karen said, before adding, "Michael Armstrong was tortured in the hope of revealing the location of his brother and lost his life. William was someone who stole money from you, and that's a strong enough motive for revenge."

"Well, thanks to him I've still got five years of my sentence left. They are shipping me out of here soon and it will be the fourth prison so far. He's not my favourite person."

"I believe someone known to you or your brother has assigned an associate to find the missing money by any means necessary." Karen stared him in the eye, unwilling to look away as he glared at her. "You may never find the money, so do yourself a favour and tell me. We need a name for the killer."

"I haven't got a clue what you're talking about. Look, I'm stuck in here, and I don't know who you think we are, but we don't have the clout you're insinuating. Yeah, I dodged my taxes, but nothing else."

"I'd disagree with you there, Paul. You forgot blackmailing a Member of Parliament and the selling of class A drugs. I think it's a little more than fudging your accounts. We need a name to stop this before any more lives are lost. I'm not bloody stupid. I know who the Harman brothers are and the extent of your criminal activity."

Harman leaned forward and rested his chubby arms on the table. His eyes darted between Ty and Karen. "Mind your own business. I'm a businessman not a criminal. We have our own way of dealing with challenges. Here's the thing, you might find that sniffing round in the wrong places could bring a whole heap of trouble to your doorstep."

"Is that a threat, Mr Harman?" Karen asked.

He shook his head. "No. But you and I both know how dangerous it is out there on the streets. Wrong time and wrong place and, well, your life can change in an instant," he said, clicking his fingers.

"Don't worry. I think we know how to look after ourselves. Let me be clear. When I find the killer, and I *will* find the killer. I will do my hardest to find any connections linking them to you. If I were you, I wouldn't get too comfortable thinking you only have five years left on your sentence. I would add a one in front of the five," Karen said, putting her notes together and leaving with Ty. Standing at the doorway, she turned round to look at Harman who stared at her with a cold, blank face. She had achieved her aim in coming here today. She knew she wouldn't get any answers, but needed the Harmans to know she was on their case and digging deeper than a former Welsh coal miner in the Rhondda Valley.

## 27

"How did it go?" Jade asked as Karen and Ty breezed into the SCU an hour after leaving HMP Leeds.

Karen nodded. "So-so. We rattled his cage, and that was my intention. I bet he was on the phone to Lee the moment we left. He's a racist, egotistical thug, and has eaten more than his fair share of pies!"

Jade and a few others laughed at Karen's assessment.

"He made a racist poke at Ty. I'm proud of him for not rising to the taunt or backing down either. Harman tried his best to be the big man but fell at the first hurdle."

A few officers nodded in Ty's direction, offering their support.

"There are a few updates for you," Ed began. "We had a call from a shopkeeper following the press appeal. He recognised the description of the BMW. On the night of Michael's murder, the shopkeeper discovered the car parked in his usual unloading spot. Out of frustration, he wrote a note and left it on the windscreen of the BMW. The next morning, he found the note crumpled on the floor and the BMW gone."

"He didn't see the driver at any point?" Karen questioned.

"I'm afraid not."

"Thanks, Ed. Anything else?" Karen asked, looking round her team.

Preet swivelled in her chair. "The mobile number you asked me to check out is a pay-as-you-go number. Whoever called Henry Beavis remained anonymous. Probably a burner phone."

Deep down, Karen suspected that would have been the case, but it bothered her. Following protocol, she had informed her boss, and the decision had been made that if Henry or any member of her team received a similar call again then they would need a risk assessment of Karen's situation both in and out of the office.

Karen thanked the team before heading off to the kitchen to rustle up a coffee. Finding the suspect was proving harder than expected. They had scoured hours of CCTV footage tracking Michael's route from his house to the industrial estate. Her team had checked and double-checked every CCTV camera, Ring doorbell, ANPR, and traffic camera. Despite their hard work, they still hadn't found a single clear image of the driver. As she sipped her coffee on the way back to her office, the elusive description of their suspect remained vague. A non-Caucasian, wearing a baseball cap, thirties to forties, broad shoulders and tall based on the CCTV footage of him retrieving the petrol can from his car. That was it. It described thousands of men up and down the country.

Settling into her seat, she switched on her computer. Tracing the money was proving just as hard. The bank accounts found in William's and Jean's names held less than fifteen thousand pounds in them. Had William spent the rest providing care for Jean? Or was the money sitting in another account yet to be discovered? Enquiries into bank accounts under the names of David or Mary Cooper had come up empty as well. Perhaps the accounts were overseas? That being the case, it would prove a challenge to uncover them.

Pulling up Google, Karen opened two tabs and placed Lee Harman in one search bar and Paul Harman in the other. News articles, business reports, and council planning announcements peppered her screen. They were mixed in with reports on the court case involving Paul. Opening a few of the entries, she scanned each page, looking for anything to help her investigation. Nothing jumped out at her. Even reports round the death of Nigel Flynn MP caused controversy. Many supporters of the Harman brothers suggested political pressure led to them being blamed for Flynn's death.

Karen scrolled through a few pages and then rubbed her eyes. One entry merged into another and, needing a break for a few seconds, she stood up and stretched her stiff back. She walked round her office a few times before pausing by the window and staring at her favourite view. It wouldn't be long before leaves fell from the trees and bony branches swayed in the chilly autumnal wind. Karen wasn't a winter person and knew conditions up north were harsh compared to London. It wasn't something she was looking forward to. She pursed her lips and nodded. Christmas would be here before she knew it and she was looking forward to spending the festive period with Zac and Summer, while finding the time to pop down to London to see her parents. She'd already decided to take Zac with her to meet them, but hadn't told him yet and laughed at the thought.

Returning to her desk, she studied her computer screen. The Connells were hardcore, streetwise, and very much in the public glare. The Harmans were more cunning and shrewd by masking their criminal activity behind legitimate businesses. Denby Construction was one of those legitimate businesses in the eyes of the authorities until William Armstrong went to the police. What followed revealed a complex network of organisations, bank accounts and associates which would leave most tax authorities scratching their heads. Many of the key players in Harmans' network had been identified, located, and questioned, with enquiries now taking place overseas. If the Harmans tasked someone to track down the money, then it wasn't from their immediate network, so it had to be hired muscle from elsewhere.

Karen picked up her phone and dialled her opposite number in Manchester. The Harmans boasted of contacts in many cities, including Manchester, but following her hunch, she needed to start there.

## 28

KAREN HUNG up the call with one of her Manchester counterparts, DCI Ben Scholes, who headed up a task force tackling organised crime in the area. It was a productive conversation where Karen discussed the Harmans and their activities at length. Scholes was familiar with the brothers and spoke in depth about a complex and sophisticated county lines network orchestrated between the Harmans and the Hasanis, a major Albanian force in the criminal underworld of Manchester, with a network of couriers supplying pubs and clubs round Manchester.

Scholes felt there was more activity between the two OCGs recently, and an undercover surveillance operation had filmed several meetings between Lee Harman and the leader of the Hasanis, Jetmir Hasani. It was a worrying development as far as Scholes was concerned because it suggested the two outfits were looking to combine their efforts to seize control of the drugs trade in the north-west, with the Harmans supplying the drugs, and the Hasanis providing the logistics and muscle.

A passing comment from Scholes had piqued Karen's interest. Greater Manchester Police had noticed a rise in punishment beatings in the criminal underworld to silence any dissenters or snitches. Intelligence suggested the Hasanis silenced and gained compliance from smaller criminal groups.

Karen had both seen and heard about the sadistic and brutal beatings between the different warring factions in and around London, especially with the influx of Eastern European organised criminal gangs which, according to the NCA, now numbered fifteen hundred in the capital alone. They came with their own brand of brutality and controlled seventy-five per cent of the sex trade in London. One such gang used a converted shipping container near the Dartford Tunnel in Essex as a torture chamber to silence their rivals.

It wasn't fresh news to Karen, but according to Scholes, the Hasanis used freelance enforcers to carry out their interrogations and punishment beatings. Scholes knew of one such freelancer who was known for cutting off the little finger on his victims' hands to force them to talk. Though his identity hadn't been confirmed, intelligence suggested Dale "Tin Snips" Cready from the Manchester area employed the method as his violent trademark. Covert officers had seen Cready in the company of Jetmir Hasani frequently.

Upon hearing that information, excitement had rippled through Karen as the first flutters had tickled her stomach. Now, she had a name for a criminal who carried a particular MO related to her two victims which sounded promising. Dale Cready was black, though from the pictures Scholes had sent across, he had lighter skin, but his size and frame matched the still photographs Karen's team had pulled off on CCTV footage. The burnt-out Honda Jazz was stolen from Manchester, and tin snips would be the perfect tool for snipping off a little finger.

The internal phone rang, shaking Karen from her thoughts.

"DCI Heath," Karen answered.

"Ma'am, we have a gentleman on the phone. He sounds quite frantic and is desperate to speak to you. Can we put the call through?"

"Sure." It took a second before the switchboard operator diverted the call through and she heard the raspy breath at the other end of the line. "Hello, DCI Heath here. I understand you want to speak to me. How can I help?"

"Help. I need help." His voice was scratchy and panicked. "I saw your press conference. They will come after me next. Help." The man's voice grew increasingly desperate.

Karen furrowed her brow and closed her eyes. It sounded like he was about to cry. "Okay, calm down. Take a few deep breaths. Who is coming after you?"

"The Harmans. They killed William. I'll be next."

"Right. Let me start by taking your name?"

"You don't understand. I don't have time. I need to keep moving as I can't let them find me. I swap my SIM card once a week and I never stay in one place long just in case I'm followed. I'm a dead man walking, and I've got nothing to do with this," the man said, desperation lacing his words as he screeched down the line.

Karen had to think fast. Robert Bagshaw sprang to mind. "Robert, is that you?"

The man sobbed down the line. "Help. I don't know what to do."

"Why don't you come into the station, and we can talk about this face to face," Karen offered.

"I can't. You don't understand. I know nothing, I swear. William gave me an envelope about a year ago when he contacted me out of the blue. Told me to keep it safe."

Karen's throat tightened. "What's in the envelope?"

"I don't know. I opened it. It's a piece of paper with some kind of code on it."

"Can you remember any of it?" Karen asked, her mind racing.

"No. I've not got it on me. I'm too scared. Oh, God. I don't want to die. This has nothing to do with me. I'm running for my life," the man spewed, before the line went dead.

Karen pulled the receiver away from her ear and stared at it for a brief second before pressing it against her ear again. "Hello? Are you still there?" Karen put the phone back in its cradle and jumped up from her seat. "Shit."

## 29

KAREN BARGED through the doors to the main SCU floor, taking many of her officers by surprise as she marched to the front of the room and stood beside the whiteboard.

"Right, team. We need to act fast, or we could have a third victim soon. I've taken a call through our switchboard. I can't be certain, but I believe it to be Robert Bagshaw. He said they are after him and he would be next."

The revelation grabbed the attention of all the officers who stopped everything they were doing, with many rising from their seats to come closer to the front as Karen continued.

"According to him, William Armstrong got in touch with him about a year ago and gave him an envelope to keep safe. After their meeting, he opened it and found a sheet of paper containing a code. He asserts his innocence and now fears for his life."

"Playing devil's advocate here," Dan interrupted, "but could it be a wind-up?"

The thought had crossed Karen's mind, but the desperation in the man's voice had sounded genuine. "I don't think so. He sounded terrified. I didn't have enough time to find out his location or convince him to come in. He might be anywhere in the country, but we need to find him. Whatever he has in his possession is putting his life in danger. The code may be the missing information we need that will lead to the money."

"Do you want me to grab the number from switchboard to do a trace?" Ed asked.

Karen nodded. "Yes, if you can, but he's using burner numbers. Thanks, Ed. I've also spoken with a DCI contact in Greater Manchester Police, DCI Ben Scholes. He gave me the low-down on active OCGs in the Greater Manchester area, and one gang in particular, the Hasanis, are teaming up with the Harmans to take control of the drug trade in Manchester. The Harmans supply, and the Hasanis distribute. But here is how it helps our case. The Hasanis use freelance enforcers. One of them is an individual called Dale "Tin Snips" Cready. He uses tin snips to cut off the little finger on his victims' hands. It's an interesting MO, and something I've only come across a few times."

"Do you think he's our man?" an officer asked.

Karen nodded. "We have no one else in the frame. Cready matches the description we have from CCTV. Light-skinned black, broad shoulders, similar height, known to hide his face by wearing a baseball cap, and wears black clothing. Michael was found in a car stolen from Manchester, and Cready plies his trade in and round Manchester. So, he could be our man."

"How do we find him?" Claire asked.

"DCI Scholes is making enquiries on our behalf. He has covert officers on the ground and will get an update for us. However, all the action is happening on our patch, so Cready is close by. Reach out to all your snouts and find out if someone matching Cready's description has been asking questions. Can someone please pass Cready's description to the shift sergeant and inspector? If any patrols spot him, they need to inform us. Do not approach him, he is a highly dangerous individual. We'll need AFOs to support us."

Karen was about to continue when a desk phone rang, and an excited officer shouted out that switchboard had the same distraught individual on the phone again. Karen dashed over to the officer and took the handset before placing it on loudspeaker for the benefit of her team.

"Hello, this is DCI Karen Heath."

A few seconds of silence followed before the sound of sobs.

"I'm here to help you. Tell me how I can do that? Is this Robert?"

The sobs turned into sniffs.

Karen remained rooted to the spot as did most of her officers, each one telepathically willing the man at the other end to say something. Anything.

"Robert, if this is you, I promise we can help. Tell me where you are. I can meet you anywhere, anytime. Even if you are at the other end of the country, I will come and meet you. Help me out here," Karen pleaded, her voice softening.

Jade nodded in approval.

"I... I... can't come in. I'm so terrified. A man claiming he's after the money visited my family. He threatened my wife and child, saying he'd cut off their fingers if I didn't come forward. If they're watching my family, they're watching *me*. It's not safe for me to leave here." His voice quivered, and his sobs seemed endless.

Karen felt helpless. She stared at the faces of her team, a sea of concerned expressions shining back at her. If she could, she would jump down the telephone line and find him. "Please. Let me help. I promise you; you will be safe with me."

"You're right. I'm Robert... Robert Bagshaw. I swear, I know nothing about this. I work as an accountant. Believe me. I didn't know what they were up to." Bagshaw sniffed and then fell silent.

Karen felt her heart hammer against her chest as thoughts tumbled through her mind. She swallowed hard, her mind going blank. She couldn't think of anything else to say. What else could she say?

"Robert, how old is your daughter?"

"Nine. Chloe is nine."

"And your wife's name is Elizabeth, right?"

He sniffed out loudly. "Yes."

"I want to protect Elizabeth and Chloe. I need to stop the man who's after you so that you, Elizabeth, and Chloe can live your lives without looking over your shoulders."

"How can you do that? I don't want to go back into witness protection. We didn't have a life being cooped up in a house, and not being able to call anyone or pop out to the local restaurant to celebrate my daughter's birthday. I don't want to get permission each time we want to go out and check in every day with law enforcement. Is that what you call living your life?"

Bagshaw had a point, though he didn't understand how those rules and procedures were in place to protect their safety.

"I understand that, Robert. We can help you get on with your life, but I need to see you," Karen said.

"I don't think I can," Bagshaw replied, hanging up.

Karen closed her eyes and tilted her head back, letting out a deep sigh. A few moments later she opened her eyes and looked at her team. They were looking to her for answers, their next steps, but she needed time to think. "Jade, can you see if we can get a location for the call? I need to update the super."

## 30

"Ma'am, have you got a moment? There's been a development," Karen said, knocking on the open door.

Detective Superintendent Laura Kelly looked up from annotating the paperwork on her desk and invited Karen in. She nodded towards a spare seat on the other side of the desk.

"We've received two calls from Robert Bagshaw, the other former accountant at Denby Construction. He sounded very distressed."

Kelly's eyes widened as she nodded, the corners of her lips turning down. "He dropped off the radar. Where is he?"

"I'm afraid he didn't say. I tried to convince him to come in, but he's running scared. He saw our press conference and the announcement about William's murder. Now, he firmly believes that they are after him."

"Who?" Kelly asked.

"The Harmans or someone connected to them. Bagshaw said, 'they have killed William. I'll be next.' And I think he meant it."

Kelly tapped her pen on her desk. "We have nothing concrete to tie the murders back to the Harmans. They are far too clever to leave a breadcrumb trail for us."

"I know, ma'am. He mentioned that someone had visited his family looking for the money. There's a strong possibility that whoever threatened his wife and child is our suspect because he said he would cut off their fingers if they didn't reveal Bagshaw's location."

Karen outlined the conversation with DCI Scholes at GMP and how Dale "Tin Snips" Cready's MO matched the injuries suffered by Michael and William Armstrong.

"How likely is it to be Cready?"

"The description fits, ma'am. We've compared images that DCI Scholes sent over to the images captured on CCTV. I'd say it's a close fit in terms of height, shape, build, and tone of skin."

"It's a serious situation we face here, Karen. If the Harmans met with the Hasanis, they probably mentioned Cready as an enforcer who achieves results. Has he got any markers?"

"Firearms."

Kelly shook her head and tossed her pen on to the desk. "Jesus, that's all we need. When we find him, you need to give officers strict instructions to stay at a safe distance and out of sight. The arrest has to be led by the AFOs."

"I agree with you, ma'am. Paul Harman is banged away, so he poses no immediate threat to us. It's his associates and contacts we need to be wary of. Lee Harman is my primary concern. Is there any chance we can tap his calls?"

Kelly shook her head. "Not without a warrant. We need something more concrete to get a snooping warrant. It's a different matter if you arrested him because we could search his phone and get his call and message logs."

Karen had suspected as much, and even if they arrested him and seized his phone, he wouldn't be stupid enough to leave any incriminating evidence on it. In her experience, most senior players in the criminal underworld used encrypted software on their phones.

Kelly reached for her keyboard. "I'm going to email ACC Jackson with an update and get his take on our next course of action. Get me more evidence, Karen. The brothers already know we are on to them, so they are going to be extra cautious and even more vigilant."

Karen rose from her chair. "Of course, ma'am. I'll do my best. Can you let me know what ACC Jackson says?"

Kelly nodded as her fingers tapped away on her keyboard, the sound of ticking and clacking echoing in Karen's ears as she left the room and headed down the corridor back to the SCU. It was getting late in the day and with time not on her side, Karen needed to do her own snooping.

## 31

KAREN PULLED up in a parking bay about fifty yards down from Lee Harman's office in Hudson Quarter, the stylish and modern development close to the railway station. With a strong black Costa coffee wedged into the drinks holder, she picked at the Danish pastry, which would have to do for dinner. The time on her dashboard read seven fifty-six p.m. The black Mercedes limo belonging to Harman's business was parked outside, so that meant Harman was still inside. Moments earlier she had called switchboard pretending to be a potential client wishing to speak to Lee Harman, only to be informed by the receptionist he was in a business meeting. When the receptionist asked for her details, Karen hung up.

With a mixture of residential town houses and commercial buildings, the street was quiet in the evening. Close by, she spotted York Brewery and what looked like a motorbike shop. A pint from York Brewery would go down a treat on a covert op, she mused. She glanced across to the banner on the railings opposite her. "A prestigious mixed-use development of one hundred and twenty-seven residences and thirty-four thousand square feet of ultra-connected commercial space," she muttered. "That's a mouthful," she laughed. "What does ultra-connected mean?" she questioned.

Karen glanced at her dashboard again. It was approaching eight fifteen p.m. She wondered how long she'd have to sit here until she glimpsed him. Her improvised stake-outs always ended up with her crawling back home in the early hours exhausted and empty-handed.

She spent the next fifteen minutes playing I spy with herself until she paused in mid-sentence as she noticed movement at the front of the building. Two burly men in suits came through the revolving doors and out on to the pavement, pausing for a moment to stare up and down the street, to check for any signs of danger. Having slid down to near horizontal over the last half hour, Karen bolted upright in her seat. One suit went round to the driver's side of the Mercedes and jumped in, starting the vehicle. The other suit lingered by the back passenger door. It was a further ten minutes before Lee Harman appeared through the revolving doors with two more casually dressed heavies following behind.

Through the inky darkness, Karen watched as Lee jumped into the rear passenger seat of the Mercedes, and the two casuals trotted off to a black Range Rover parked behind it. Moments later they pulled away. Karen dipped down into her seat again before starting her car to follow at a discreet distance.

The Mercedes dipped and darted from main roads to side streets, closely followed by the Range Rover. She realised the drivers of both vehicles were trained in the art of surveillance and defensive driving. It was a common tactic used to lose a tail or alter a journey so a potential assailant couldn't plan and mount a strike. The Mercedes slowed and stopped outside a bar where Lee Harman and his entourage stepped out and disappeared down a side alley next to it.

The Sands Bar was a well-known haunt for criminals, so Karen wasn't about to enter. She would have to settle for observing from the safety of her car. Over the next thirty minutes several suspicious-looking individuals arrived and disappeared down the same alley, entering the bar through the fire exit. After another forty five minutes, Lee Harman reappeared with a few of the individuals who had arrived after him. A slim brunette hung on his arm. Dressed in a tight figure-hugging black dress, her heels clipped on the pavement as she tottered alongside him. He shook hands with many of the men before getting back in his car and driving off. That tickled her Spidey senses, but seeing Harman holding a briefcase concerned her more. He hadn't been carrying one when he'd entered. Karen took a few photos on her phone before starting her car and following the Mercedes, only to find it returning to Hudson Quarter and Harman's penthouse apartment. Harman and the brunette stepped from the vehicle accompanied by two minders, disappearing through the revolving doors before the Mercedes and Range Rover sped away, their tyres squealing on the tarmac.

Karen gasped when she realised Harman wasn't carrying the briefcase. It was still in the Mercedes. Karen started her car and shot off after them. She trailed through the narrow streets as they criss-crossed roads and sped up round slow-moving vehicles. Unsure whether they had spotted her, she kept her distance, indicating left as they did at the next traffic light. The lights turned red as she approached.

"Shit. Shit." Karen hissed. Checking for oncoming traffic, Karen darted through the red light and turned left. She saw the rear brake lights of the Range Rover about one hundred yards ahead of her, and the Mercedes about fifty yards further on past that. The Range Rover had slowed to a snail's pace, and as Karen moved into the middle of the road to get a better view of the Mercedes, she noticed it had come to a stop. A dark figure, dressed in black with a dark baseball cap, stood beside the Mercedes as the briefcase was handed to them through an open window. The figure turned and darted off down a side road.

Tension stiffened Karen's muscles. She wanted to race after the figure, but doing so would cause her to run into Harman's heavies. She slapped the heel of her palm on the steering wheel in frustration. *They're good. Very good.* They had cleverly positioned the Range Rover to block any traffic behind it while the transaction took place. With oncoming traffic scuppering any chances of Karen passing, the recipient of the briefcase had enough time to make their escape.

Both of Harman's vehicles sped away, the red tail lights disappearing into the distance. Karen knew there was no point in chasing them as she slowed to the spot where she had seen the dark figure. She glanced round. Nothing. Her thoughts turned to the shadowy figure. Was that Dale Cready? And what was in the briefcase? A firearm or money?

## 32

PULLING into the car park nearest to her station block, Karen parked beside Jade, who was at the rear of her car, grabbing a bag from her boot.

She was running late, having taken an early morning call from Grant Chilvers, the social welfare officer looking after Jean Armstrong. The news he'd shared excited her, and she'd promised to get back to him later this morning.

Karen stepped out of her vehicle and threw on her jacket before yawning. "Morning, Jade."

"Morning," Jade replied, shutting her boot and walking beside Karen.

"I did a bit of unofficial snooping on Lee Harman last night, and I might have got close to Dale Cready, though I can't be certain."

Jade looked astonished as she glanced at Karen in confusion. "You followed him?"

Karen nodded.

"Christ, Karen. When will you ever learn? Your unofficial surveillance keeps getting you in trouble. And following Lee Harman? Are you looking to die early?" Jade said, shaking her head.

"I was careful. The super won't allow a surveillance operation or a telephone tap unless I come to her with evidence. What else was I supposed to do? I followed him after he left his office. He goes everywhere with a strong security detail. Two with him, and another two following in a backup car." Karen continued to tell Jade about Lee Harman's visit to the Sands Bar with several other suspicious-looking individuals.

"Associates? Or a rival firm?" Jade asked.

"I'm not sure. Can you run a search on the owners of the Sands Bar? It was a brief meet, so I'm not sure what happened inside," Karen said as she pulled open the door to her building and swiped her card on the internal doors. She headed to the SCU and spoke about Lee appearing with a briefcase and it being passed on to someone else in a well-executed handover.

"You think it was Cready?" Jade asked, stopping by the door to Karen's office.

Karen shrugged. "I'm not sure. Could be. What concerns me was the contents of the briefcase. Firearms, drugs, even cash."

"Still doesn't help our case. We could tug his chain and pull him in, but it would work against us. He'd cover his tracks knowing we're on to him or complain about police harassment."

"Yep, he's a slippery git. Based on DCI Scholes's feedback I think we need to focus on finding Cready to begin with. Bringing down Lee Harman would be a bonus, but Grant Chilvers called me this morning. In one of her lucid moments, Jean Armstrong mentioned a tall dark-skinned man hurt William and made him cry."

"Cready," Jade suggested.

Karen nodded. "I think so. Send someone over to meet with Grant and show Jean a picture of Dale Cready. Jean was the only one who saw William's killer. We know she has issues with her memory and speech, but if we can catch her in another lucid moment when she IDs Cready, then it's a major step forward for us even though Jean wouldn't stand up in court as a credible witness, and Cready's defence team would leverage the dementia angle big time."

"Will do," Jade replied, heading back to the main SCU floor.

Karen hung up her coat and then flicked through the mail on her desk while firing up her computer.

"Karen, do you have a moment?" Preet asked.

"Sure, come in," Karen said as she admired Preet's dress sense. Preet had a knack of looking smart but casual, and with minimal make-up, her dark hair and big brown eyes complemented her smooth and fair complexion. Every time Karen looked at her, Preet reminded her of the stunning Bollywood actress Priyanka Chopra.

"A few of us have been looking at the Paul Harman court case. We've uncovered evidence of witness intimidation. In particular, a local councillor, Arjun Kumar, received death threats when he chaired a planning meeting about the construction of a commercial building by Denby Construction. He denied planning approval, which didn't go down too well." Preet handed Karen a statement from the file. "As you'll see, Mr Kumar first received a large envelope of cash through his letter box at home. Five grand in cash. It was labelled, 'A gift for you'. He then received an anonymous telephone call. A male caller who claimed to be the one who'd posted the money through his letter box. Mr Kumar was told that as the chair of the planning committee, if he approved the planning application, they would drop another twenty grand through his letter box. No questions asked."

Karen scanned the details. It sounded like a classic case of attempted bribery. The threats became more serious when someone set Mr Kumar's car on fire on his front drive. According to the paperwork in Karen's hand, Mr Kumar had to move his family to a gated complex which had twenty-four-hour security at the main entrance to the estate, regular foot patrols, and CCTV installed with a panic button.

"Okay, thanks, Preet. Can you call? I'll head over and see him now."

Preet nodded and left the room.

Karen returned to the statement, reading one particular line over several times with keen interest. Mr Kumar was certain that two burly white males in a Range Rover frequently followed him.

## 33

*The gates are as impressive as what lays beyond*, Karen thought as she edged the nose of her car to within inches of the wrought-iron gates with splendid iron spear finials which ran along the top. Two security guards appeared from the sentry box and approached, one smiling, the other holding back with a clipboard and a miserable face.

"Morning. Detective Chief Inspector Heath to see Mr Kumar. He's expecting me," Karen announced, holding her ID out for the first guard to see.

He leaned forward and studied her details before stepping back and nodding at "miserable face", who remained po-faced as he headed back into his box.

Seconds later, the gates opened, and a guard gave Karen directions. With sprawling grassy areas and an array of town houses, detached houses, and luxury apartments, it reminded her of Repton Park close to where she used to live, a former mental asylum converted into an exclusive residential complex in Woodford, Essex, where wealthy business owners, premiership footballers, and models sought privacy and safety.

She followed the tree-lined road as it snaked through the development until she found the address and spotted an Asian man dressed in a crisp open-neck white shirt and dark grey trousers.

Karen switched off her ignition and stepped from her car before coming round to meet the man. "Arjun Kumar?"

"Yes. Detective Chief Inspector, a pleasure to meet you. I understand you wanted a word with me?"

"Yes. I won't take up too much of your time."

"Well, considering it's nice out today, shall we walk and talk? I like to stretch my legs a few times a day and walk round the grounds."

Karen smiled and nodded before crossing the road with Arjun and stepping on to the grass. Fields stretched for as far as the eye could see. On the outskirts of the city centre, the development exuded a calm and relaxing feel with mature trees creating shady spots. Karen envisioned families gathering under them for impromptu summer picnics. She'd rather pick one of those spots and enjoy a glass of wine and listen to music on headphones or indulge in a good book, both of which she loved to do but rarely found the time.

"Thank you for seeing me at short notice. I am the SIO investigating the murder of two brothers. One of which was an accountant at Denby Construction."

Kumar nodded as he rubbed his chin and stared down at the grass. "Yes, I saw that on the news. Very tragic. Denby Construction. I guessed that's why you're here."

Karen breathed in the fresh smell of cut grass which lingered in the air. "Yes. This is strictly between you and me. We believe the Harmans may be connected to the murder of both brothers. We suspect that an enforcer from Manchester committed the murders. The Harmans might have hired the enforcer to track down a large amount of cash that William Armstrong had stolen."

"I wouldn't put it past them. They made my life hell, and I nearly lost my family and my life," Kumar said.

"You believe they were sending you cash to push through their planning application?"

Kumar nodded. "Hundred per cent. I gave the money to the police, as I wanted no part in their dealings. When I didn't play ball, two men stopped me a few times both near my home and office. I wasn't roughed up or anything, but their attitude was very intimidating and subtle." Kumar tutted as he thought back to those occasions. "They suggested there were nasty people out there who, if they didn't get their way, would make my life very uncomfortable. They said it would be terrible if a passing car knocked my daughter down while she crossed the road."

"I know about your car being torched on your front drive. I read the report. Did anything else happen?" Karen asked.

Kumar nodded. "I had a few threatening phone calls. Some were completely silent. But I knew someone was at the other end of the line. Then there were a few where the caller mentioned places I'd been to in recent days. I soon realised I was being followed."

"Do you believe the Harmans were behind this?" Karen asked.

"Without a doubt. I rejected their planning application. The project would have cost millions and been very profitable for them, but the proposed site contained a preservation order on a historic copse of trees. The project couldn't go ahead. It was a simple decision as far as I was concerned."

"Was there any other tangible evidence to link it back to the Harmans?"

Kumar fell silent as he continued to walk round the grounds, his eyes drifting off into the distance. It was a few moments before he nodded and pursed his lips in frustration and anger. "I remember driving past Hudson Quarter one day and the men who had stopped me a few times were outside the address where the Harmans have their office, and they were shaking hands with both Harman brothers." Kumar sighed before pulling his mobile from his back pocket and opening his gallery of photos. He scrolled through before finding one and showing it to Karen.

Karen stopped and took Kumar's phone from him. The screen showed a picture of the Harman brothers standing outside the same building she had scoped the night before, and they were smiling and shaking hands with two thickset, broad-shouldered men in bomber jackets and jeans. Karen looked perplexed as she looked at Kumar. "This wasn't in your report to the police?"

Kumar shook his head. "I couldn't risk telling the police about it. I'm not sure how seriously it would have been taken, but I'm telling you now as a senior detective on the case. I already fear for myself and my family. It would have annoyed the Harmans further, and what would have happened after that? They are not people to be messed with. I had to think of my family. It's the reason I kept quiet about this and didn't report it."

Karen didn't blame him for being scared. Most people would be in that situation. In this secure environment he could at least protect his family, but she knew the Harmans could get to him if they wanted to. Yes, the development had tall railings and brick walls surrounding it, but it wouldn't take much to scale them, or to pretend to be a courier firm with a delivery, even a utility worker. "Do you mind sending me this picture and any others that you have?"

Kumar nodded as he took his phone back. Karen pulled out Cready's photograph from her bag. "Have you ever seen this man before?"

Kumar studied it intently. His eyes narrowed as his brow furrowed. He shook his head. "No. Who is he?"

"He's our key suspect in the double homicide."

Kumar and Karen had followed a long loop round the grounds and were in sight of her car as they returned.

"DCI Heath, I'll leave you here as I'd like to continue my walk and then attend a meeting in town. I appreciate you coming to see me, and please let me know of any developments."

"Of course I will, Mr Kumar. Thank you so much for your time. Here's my card. Can you forward those photos to my phone? And you now have my direct contact details in case you think of anything else that may be of use, or need to reach me in an emergency," Karen said, before fishing her car keys out of her bag and walking back to her car. The images she had seen on Kumar's phone were helpful. Though it was dark, she wondered if those in the photographs had been the crew driving the Mercedes and Range Rover the night before.

## 34

A TEXT from Jade relating to the Bagshaw family had Karen racing back. There were only two things on Karen's mind upon returning to the office. Finding both Cready and Robert Bagshaw. Her conversation with Mr Kumar had reinforced her belief that the Harmans were dangerous individuals with menacing influence who got what they wanted, and if they didn't, would dish out their own punishment and threats. Cready was proving elusive to uncover. She knew he would still be in the city; his work wasn't complete. He could be five minutes away and yet Karen wasn't in touching distance of capturing him. But it wasn't all bad news as she rushed through the doors to the SCU to be greeted by her excited officers.

Dan yelled across the floor they had caught Cready entering the Armstrongs' property on the night of William's murder.

Karen stalled, not knowing whether to get an update on Jade's news or Dan's. Deciding both were important, she hurried over to Dan's desk first as a few other officers rose from their seats and gathered round Dan's desk. With the recent developments, a buzz of energy filled the room.

"What have we got?" Karen said, placing a hand on Dan's shoulder and leaning over.

"Following our appeal, we got dashcam footage from an Uber driver. He had parked further up the road and was taking a break ahead of picking up his next customers who had booked him for an airport run. The customers heading to the airport just so happen to live on the same street as the Armstrongs. Sharif, the driver, had poured some coffee from his flask when he saw a suspicious figure appear from the shadows and walk over to the Armstrongs' property."

Karen felt a lightness in her chest as she bit down on a smile. A racing heartbeat felt like her insides were vibrating. "Let's have a look then."

Dan pressed the play button on his screen and let the footage roll. Those gathered round him fell silent, their eyes firmly fixed on the screen. The camera provided a view down the street and luckily for Karen, no one had parked in front of Sharif's Toyota Prius, so it afforded her an uninterrupted view of the Armstrongs' house. All seemed quiet in the street for the first thirty seconds and then a figure appeared from behind a row of parked cars wearing a yellow hi-vis jacket and carrying a clipboard. Even though the image was dark, with the help of a nearby street light, it was enough to identify a profile matching Dale "Tin Snips" Cready as he passed beneath it.

Unable to control her excitement, Karen punched the air. The evidence placed Cready at the scene on the night of the murder. Along with the team, she continued to watch the footage. Cready went to the door and after a few moments the shaded silhouette of William Armstrong answered it. A brief conversation followed before William closed the door a bit and disappeared back inside. They watched as Cready waited a moment before stepping through the unlocked door and closing it behind him.

"Bloody brilliant," Karen whispered. "Didn't Sharif think it was odd seeing a utility worker turn up late in the evening?"

Dan shook his head. "Sharif thought nothing of it as there was a big E.ON logo on the back of the jacket. He thought there was a problem at the property and the owners had called the electricity company."

"Did Sharif see Cready leave?" Karen asked.

"No. He was only there for another fifteen minutes before setting off to pick up his customers."

"Well, we know he was there witnessing Cready, and that's the main thing. Dale Cready murdered William Armstrong and we can place him at the scene during the window when Izzy estimated the time of death. That's good enough for me," Karen said.

"We just need to find the bastard now," one of her officers said. A sentiment many officers agreed with as they nodded.

"I can't find any phone records for the past eight months in Bagshaw's name," Ed chipped in, deciding to perch on a neighbouring desk. "He's probably been using a pay-as-you-go phone since then. His bank records show little in the way of transactions in the past two months. I can only assume he has access to other funds."

"Do you have an update on where he might be staying?" Karen said, looking at Ed and Jade. "He has to be a priority for us. We need to locate him."

Ed continued. "Yes. He's rented several properties over the last few years. Moved round a lot. Never in one place longer than six months. From what I can tell, his details are linked to two rental properties. A small bungalow in Rawcliffe and a static caravan in Weir Caravan Park east of the city. I asked local units to attend both addresses this morning. We found Bagshaw's wife and daughter at the caravan park. They were terrified. Elizabeth, his wife, said Bagshaw went out this morning. Didn't say where he was going or what time he would be back."

"I've authorised the move of his wife and daughter to a safer location. I hope that's okay?" Jade said.

Karen nodded. "Perfect."

"We have Bagshaw's current mobile number," Jade said, handing a yellow Post-it to Karen. "I asked his wife to text Robert, telling him they were safe and with the police. I didn't want him to come back to the caravan and panic if they weren't there."

Karen chewed on her bottom lip as she thought things through. Bagshaw was running scared, but she needed to reach out to him. She pulled her mobile out of her pocket and dialled his number. When it rang out, she cursed, wondering if he had already discarded his phone and swapped in a new SIM card. Regardless, she sent him a text asking him to get in touch and hoped he would get it.

## 35

AN HOUR HAD PASSED, and still no reply from Robert Bagshaw. Karen glanced between her computer and her mobile phone on her desk every few minutes, hoping and praying that Bagshaw would reach out to her. His situation was precarious. He had limited options and was isolated with nowhere to go. She hoped that, knowing his family was safe with the police, he would get in touch. As the minutes slipped by, Karen grew increasingly doubtful.

Having kicked off her shoes, she rose from her chair and padded round her office, feeling the softness of the carpet beneath her feet. She glanced round feeling helpless. Trying to keep herself busy as her impatience grew, she'd rearranged the books on her bookshelf several times, and readjusted the prints on the walls even though they weren't wonky. Everything possible was being done to locate Bagshaw and Cready. The team had circulated both of their images to officers on patrol with strict instructions to give Cready a wide berth until armed officers were in position to make an arrest.

Karen's phone rang and vibrated on her desk. She rushed to it, her heart in her mouth, hoping it was Bagshaw only to see Mr Kumar's number pop up on her screen. She pursed her lips in surprise.

"Mr Kumar. I wasn't expecting to hear from you so soon. Is everything okay?"

"Yes, but I need a word with you." It sounded like he was out and about as the noise of passing traffic drowned out his voice. "As I pulled out of the gates on my journey into town, I spotted a black Audi A6 parked across the road. It had two men in it. At first I paid little attention to it, but as I drove off, they followed me for most of my journey before disappearing from my rear-view mirror."

"Did you get a look at the occupants?" Karen asked.

"Not clearly. Two white males. The side windows had privacy glass, so it made the inside of the car quite dark. I took a photograph of the registration details when they slowed behind me at the lights."

"Can you send it to me? It's probably nothing to worry about, but I'm glad you take your safety seriously," Karen said, attempting to downplay the experience to allay his fears.

"I'm sending it through now on WhatsApp. I have to dash. My meeting is about to start." Kumar thanked her before hanging up.

A few seconds later, the photograph popped up on her WhatsApp. She opened it and studied the image. Kumar was right. The inside of the car was too dark to make out any distinguishable features of the occupants. Karen sat down at her desk and logged into the PNC to run a check on the registration number. It took seconds for the data to come back and with a further few clicks the owner of the car popped up on the screen. Karen ground her teeth as she jumped from her seat and slipped on her shoes. She hurried through the building and headed to the station car park to grab the keys to a pool car.

---

THIRTY MINUTES LATER, Karen stormed through the revolving doors of Hudson Quarter and, ignoring the polite objections from the ground-floor receptionist, she flashed her warrant card towards the woman, hit the button on the elevator and took it up to Harman's reception. The doors chimed open. She stepped into reception to be greeted by the same receptionist she had seen on her last visit. Ignoring her as well, Karen marched down the hallway to Harman's office. The sound of Karen approaching alerted the bodyguards guarding their boss.

The men stiffened and pulled their shoulders back, blocking the doorway with their wide frames as Karen turned the corner.

Karen held up her warrant card. "I suggest you get your fat arses out of the way, or I'll have you arrested for obstructing a police officer, and trust me I'm in no mood to be pissed off."

The bodyguards glared at her, neither averting their gaze. They stood their ground. With the receptionist having caught up, they pinned Karen in from both sides, which only incensed her further as her body tensed and heat flushed through her body. Her face reddened as she glared at the bodyguards, her lips flattening into a thin line.

"I won't bloody tell you again. Move aside or I will have you arrested for impeding a double murder investigation," Karen yelled.

The door opened behind the heavies and Lee Harman appeared. "What the fuck is going on?" he hissed.

"We have an uninvited visitor," one of the heavies growled.

Upon seeing Karen, Lee Harman relaxed and rolled his eyes before offering her a curt smile. "Calm down, gentlemen. She's harmless. Couldn't fight your way out of a wet paper bag, could you, constable?" he teased. "Let her through boys." Harman turned and disappeared back into his office, leaving the door wide open.

The two men separated, their eyes twitching with fury as Karen walked between them and into Harman's office. She walked to his desk, her shoes clip-clopping on the tiled floor. Harman was already seated by the time she reached him.

"What is it you want, officer? I'm a very busy man, but I will say you do like to make an entrance," he said, laughing.

Karen pulled out her phone and retrieved the image Kumar had sent her. "Do you know these individuals?" she asked, turning the phone so Harman could see.

He narrowed his eyes as he studied the small picture. He grimaced and shook its head. "No, I'm afraid not. Should I?"

"You tell me. They were driving a black Audi A6 registered to your company. That suggests they are your employees."

Harman leaned back in his chair and swivelled from side to side, seemingly in no hurry to reply. "I have a lot of employees. I don't know every single one. Did you ever consider the possibility that someone might have cloned the plates?"

Karen smiled back. "I did. I checked. There are no reports of the registration being cloned or committing any traffic offences. So it's unlikely. A couple of your heavies followed Mr Kumar this morning. He's a councillor you'll be very familiar with because he chaired the committee that turned down one of your planning applications." Karen stepped forward and rested her hands on the desk. "It's an offence to cause harassment, alarm, or distress. I suggest it would be in your best interest to have a word with your *employees,* because if it continues, they could spend six months at His Majesty's pleasure. Perhaps they wouldn't be too keen on the idea and may cut a deal and spill the beans on who you really are and what you do." Karen stepped back, not averting her gaze from Harman.

"Are you threatening me?" Harman growled through gritted teeth.

"Not at all. It's called proactive policing. Nip the problem in the bud before it gets too big. I'm all in favour of ripping out the poisonous weeds. You're the kind of man who enjoys getting his own way, but not any more. Not on my patch. I'll make sure of that." Karen turned and walked away, leaving Lee Harman seething silently in his chair.

---

KAREN SMILED to herself as she made the journey back to the station. She had dealt with the crime bosses in London and though another level up from the Connells, he didn't put her off. Hardened criminals and street rats had pointed guns and knives at her, but she'd never backed down despite being scared.

Her visit had rattled Harman. When his lids had flickered, she'd seen it in his eyes. That first glimmer of doubt suggested he wasn't in control, nor could he control her.

Karen slowed at the lights, her fingers tapping on the steering wheel in time to the song on her radio. There was so much for her to do, and the day was flying by. As the lights turned green, she pulled off, crossing the junction. She didn't register the car travelling at speed through the red light to her left until it was too late. It clipped her left rear nearside quarter panel, sending her car into a three-hundred-and-sixty-degree spin. Karen gripped the steering wheel as her view became fuzzy and disorientated. Her mouth ran dry as her heart thundered in her chest. Gripping the steering wheel hard, her knuckles went white and her eyes fixed wide in terror.

It was as if the world had gone silent for a few moments as her focus sharpened. She blinked hard and unbuckled her seat belt before staggering from her car. Drivers raced from their vehicles to check on her. Other than being shaken and disorientated, she felt fine. She glanced round, looking for the offending vehicle. But it was gone, having sped off from the scene, just fragments of broken headlight glass and trim littering the pavement. With her hands shaking, Karen retrieved her two-way radio from her handbag and gripped the unit hard before calling it in.

## 36

AN HOUR LATER, Karen sat in the SCU surrounded by her team as they listened to her recollection of the accident. Ambulance staff had arrived and checked her over before giving her a clean bill of health. Other than being a little shaken, she was unscathed. A recovery truck had taken the car away and, following a debrief with officers at the scene, a patrol car had driven her back to the station.

Detective Superintendent Laura Kelly came through the doors and made her way over to the huddle round Karen. The officers moved to one side as she approached. "How are you feeling?"

"I'm okay, ma'am. The car came off worse than me."

Kelly smiled. "That's good. Did you catch a glimpse of the driver?"

Karen shook her head. "It happened too quickly. I saw a glimpse of the car from the corner of my eye. I didn't have time to react before it slammed into me."

"They found the car a mile away. Burnt out, I'm afraid. It was reported stolen four days ago. A joyrider I expect."

"Possibly, ma'am. I was returning after seeing Lee Harman. A couple of his heavies have been intimidating Mr Kumar, a local councillor. They drove a car registered to the Harman's business. Having checked the reg on the PNC, I visited him to present the evidence. I made it clear intimidation and harassment could lead to criminal charges."

Kelly raised a brow. "I guess he didn't take too kindly to your visit?"

"No, ma'am. I'm wondering if this was a deliberate act on his part to scare me off?" Karen replied.

"That's nothing more than speculation, Karen. But it's plausible. Get yourself off home and relax." Kelly smiled before heading off.

Jade waited for Kelly to disappear. "Do you think Harman was behind this?"

"It could have been a random joyrider. It could happen to anyone. My gut instinct tells me Harman was behind it. He's used to getting his own way and doesn't like people interfering in his business. I stirred up a hornet's nest when I went in there. This is his way of telling me to back off."

Karen got to her feet and grabbed her handbag. "I'm not scared of him. I've been there before. If he was behind it that just shows how much we've got under his skin. We all need to be vigilant," Karen said, looking round at her officers. "It might be over the top, but the Harmans are in a different league and wouldn't think twice about hurting any one of us. So be careful."

A murmur of agreement rumbled round the room as Karen left and headed to Zac's.

---

ZAC HAD TAKEN work home with him earlier in the day and was there when she rang the doorbell.

"You do like the limelight, don't you?" Zac teased as he opened the door and kissed her on the cheek. "News of your accident spread like wildfire round the base. Are you okay?" he asked, closing the door and heading to the lounge. He grabbed the remote and turned the volume down on the TV before logging off his laptop and putting it back in its case.

"I'm fine. The pool car isn't," she replied. "That will be out of action at the body shop for a few weeks. Where's Summer?"

"She headed off to the park with Lottie about half an hour ago," Zac replied, checking the time on his phone. He opened the Find My app to check Summer's current location. It updated one minute ago and confirmed she was close to the park.

"Someone said it was a joyrider? Did you get a look at him?"

"No. It happened too quickly, and the car was gone before I got out. Call me a cynic, but I don't think it was a joyrider. I think Lee Harman was warning me off." Karen spent the next ten minutes outlining her visit to Lee Harman and how she'd left him infuriated.

"Do you think he could have pulled it off so quickly? I mean, within twenty minutes of you leaving his office you're hit by a speeding car. I can't see it myself," Zac said.

When Zac put it that way, it *did* sound ridiculous to her. But there was something niggling her. Zac got up and went to the kitchen to grab the white wine from the fridge. Karen followed and wrapped her arms round him from behind as he retrieved two wine glasses from an overhead cupboard. She closed her eyes and breathed in his scent as she listened to the sound of wine glugging from the bottle and into the glasses. He turned in her embrace and kissed her again before offering her a glass.

"Here, get this down your neck," he said.

Karen accepted and took a sip, savouring the sharp coolness of the wine on her tongue as it trickled down her throat. "Ooh, perfect. I fancy something simple for dinner tonight. How about bacon and scrambled eggs on toast?"

Zac nodded just as his phone rang. Placing his glass down on the kitchen worktop, he headed back into the lounge to grab his phone from the coffee table. There was silence for a few moments until he raised his voice.

"Summer, calm down. Tell me exactly what happened," he said, trying his hardest to keep his voice steady and calm as he raced back into the kitchen and stared at Karen, who looked equally alarmed. "Stay where you are. Make sure there are people round you," he paused for a moment, waiting for Summer's reply. "Good. Don't move from there. We are on our way. Stay on the line. I'll send the police to you right away."

"Karen, now!" he shouted as he rushed from the kitchen to the hall to grab his car keys.

"What's happened?" Karen said, concern tainting her voice as she put the glass down and ran after him.

"Someone has snatched Lottie."

## 37

Zac screeched to a halt behind a long line of police vehicles as officers swarmed the area. He had called in the emergency as he left, setting the wheels in motion for a large-scale police operation.

A missing or abducted child was the highest priority incident for any force across the country, and with Lottie being connected to the family of a serving officer, the response was immediate and extensive. York police had diverted every available officer to the scene. A police helicopter from NPAS had arrived minutes earlier following Zac's request and was circling overhead in large loops as they trained their camera on the narrow streets below.

Karen and Zac raced from his vehicle to the focal point where most of the officers had gathered. A female officer among them had her arm draped round Summer as she sobbed uncontrollably. Upon seeing her dad, Summer pulled away from the officer and ran into his arms, burying her head into his chest, her muffled and strained screams pulling on everyone's heartstrings. Karen stroked the back of Summer's hair as she tried to soothe the poor girl.

Zac placed his hands on Summer's shoulders and took a step back before placing a kiss on her forehead. "You're okay, baby. You're safe. Tell me what happened?" he asked softly. Summer's chest heaved as she gasped for breath, tears streaking her face, her eyes puffy and red.

"We... We... were walking along here towards the entrance of the park... and..." Summer's words stuttered as panic gripped her again. Her body trembled as her shoulders shivered.

"Take your time, darling. Take your time. You're doing really well," Zac reassured her, wiping away her tears with his thumbs.

Karen remained silent, giving Zac and Summer the space they needed.

Summer took a deep breath and continued. "We were about to go into the park and a white van pulled up. The side door opened, and two men jumped out and... and... grabbed Lottie... We both screamed. I didn't know what to do. They pulled Lottie into the van, shut the door and..." Tears cascaded from Summer's eyes as she wailed.

"Did you get a good look at the two men?" Zac asked.

Summer shook her head.

"Were they white? Black? Asian?"

"White. Both men were white."

Zac nodded as he rubbed her shoulders. "Roughly what age? Young, perhaps in their twenties, or were they older like me?" Zac knew his questions were confusing his daughter, but every shred of information would help officers on the ground to find the van, the abductors, and Lottie.

Summer shrugged. "I don't know, Dad. They weren't as old as you. They looked younger."

Zac wrapped his arms round his daughter and held her tight as he nodded in Karen's direction.

Karen darted off, barking into her radio, relaying information back to the control room, before updating officers on the scene. Karen grabbed her phone and called Jade.

"Jade, it's Karen. We've got a situation."

"I know, I've just heard. It's Summer's friend, right?" Jade said.

"Yes. Two men in a white van have abducted her, two of which were Caucasian. I don't know about the driver's description. They headed off in a northerly direction. Can you get on to the council CCTV unit and check to see if they picked up the van on any cameras? I'm pretty certain they would have. We need to find out which direction the abductors headed in. Grab a reg off the footage and set up an ANPR ping. This is urgent. It's a high-risk case."

Karen listened as Jade relayed those instructions on to officers round her.

"How is Summer?" Jade said.

Karen sighed. "She is a mess. I don't know if this was random or deliberate. Why only Lottie? Why didn't they grab both girls? If they were paedos, they would have grabbed both."

"It's high-risk if it was random," Jade remarked. "Paedophiles normally groom young girls over time rather than snatch them. It's much rarer for them to snatch someone unless they are violent offenders."

Karen agreed with Jade's assessment.

"Is there anything else you want me to do?"

"I need to stay here with Zac and Summer. Do you mind going to see Lottie's parents and breaking the news to them?"

"Of course not. I'll head there now and take Bel with me."

"Brilliant. Thanks. While there, be subtle with it, but ask a few questions about who she's been hanging round with, names of any new friends, even boyfriends. Search her bedroom, too. Let's cross off all bases and be thorough with it."

"Got it. Can you send me through her number, and I'll trace the provider and set up a ping on her phone?"

"Yes. I'll get it from Summer for you now. Let me know how you get on with Lottie's parents," Karen said before hanging up.

## 38

NIGHTFALL HAD COME, and the force was on high alert. Officers combed the streets, and scrutinised CCTV footage from every source. Each passing hour meant another fraught and upsetting hour for Lottie's parents.

Jade and Belinda were still with them and providing Karen with constant updates. Triangulation on Lottie's phone had last picked up a signal three miles from her home. With the cell site data suggesting the phone was moving further north and away from town, they'd deployed extra resources to the area. NPAS provided the extra aerial search capability they needed to scour the city and the countryside beyond the city boundary.

Karen had returned to Zac's and spent the last few hours providing whatever support she could to the pair. Lottie's abduction had left Summer shaken and traumatised. Specially trained officers had arrived at Zac's to interview her, covering similar questions to those Zac had asked but in more detail. Summer had found the entire experience difficult, her answers being broken by further bouts of crying, and Zac looking on. He was there as her father, not a police officer, so felt the pain and helplessness any parent would experience in that situation.

Karen stepped out of the lounge and headed into the kitchen, closing the door behind her before calling Jade. "How are they coping?" she asked, checking the time on the wall clock and grimacing. It was gone ten p.m. Lottie had been gone for over four hours.

"They are not coping well," Jade replied. "Sandra, her mum, is in bits. Brad, Lottie's Dad, swings from moments of being quiet to rage. He's desperate to get out there and look for her. We've had to stop him twice from leaving the house. I won't even repeat what he said he would do to the people who abducted her. How is Summer?"

"Deeply traumatised. She will need professional help to process it. Kids of this age often bottle up their emotions and experiences because they don't know how to process them."

"And Zac?"

"He hasn't left her side. Summer is curled into him. She goes from moments of being awake and crying to dozing off. Let me know if you hear anything," Karen said.

"Likewise," Jade replied before hanging up.

Karen came out of the kitchen and went back into the lounge. Summer and Zac were both dozing. She sat on the coffee table in front of them and tapped Zac on the knee. His bloodshot eyes shot open as he glanced round the room, tuning in his senses. "Why don't you stretch your legs? I'll sit with Summer."

Zac yawned and blinked hard to wake up. "Thanks. Any news?"

Karen shook her head.

Summer stirred as Zac stood. "Dad, where are you going?"

"I'm going to the loo and making a hot drink for both of us. Karen wants to sit with you."

Karen slid into the warm spot that Zac had left behind. Summer leaned against Karen and offered her a weak smile. "How are you holding up?"

Summer shrugged. "I don't know. I keep seeing it over and over again every time I close my eyes. It happened so fast. I've never seen Lottie look so scared as they dragged her away. I'll never forget the look in her eyes when she looked at me. I should have done more."

Karen took Summer's hand and squeezed it. "Listen, you have done nothing wrong. Everyone in your situation would have the same feelings. It's such a shock to the system. It's natural to freeze. Our minds can't think fast enough. I've experienced the same thing occasionally. When events happen that fast, our bodies can't react as quickly as we'd like them to."

"Really?" Summer asked, looking at Karen.

Karen's heart melted when she saw the pain in Summer's face. She looked like a little lost girl searching for reassurance and support in Karen's eyes. Karen threw her arm round Summer and pulled her in close. "Promise. Your reaction was perfectly normal. The main thing is you are safe."

"But Lottie isn't."

Karen nodded. "We'll find her."

Zac poked his head round the door with two mugs and saw Summer falling asleep in Karen's arms. He winked at Karen and mouthed, *I love you*, before heading back into the kitchen.

Karen stroked Summer's hair. She knew Summer was worried about her friend, but she needed to rest, too.

Somewhere deep within her senses Karen felt a tickle on her leg. It was a few moments before her eyes flicked open. Her vision appeared fuzzy, and the ceiling light felt like a glowing orb stabbing her eyes. She had fallen asleep but wasn't sure for how long. Summer was fast asleep beside her, wrapped up in Karen's arm, which felt numb, and Zac lay asleep on the sofa opposite them. With her other hand she reached for her phone and saw Jade's name on the screen.

"Hi," Karen whispered.

"We have found Lottie. She is alive. A motorist found her wandering seven miles north of the city centre. Officers are bringing her back now."

"Was she hurt?"

"No, just distressed and grubby."

Karen felt the relief wash over her as her tense muscles relaxed. She closed her eyes and said a silent prayer of gratitude. "Thank God. That's fantastic news. I'll let Zac and Summer know. She is asleep beside me," Karen said in a hushed tone. "Are you going to wait for Lottie?"

"Yes. I want to make sure Lottie and her parents are okay. We'll need to interview Lottie first thing tomorrow morning, but for now I think the family needs to be reunited and I'll get a FLO sorted out right away. I'll make sure there's a police presence for the next day or two."

"Definitely. Thanks to the both of you for putting in the extra hours to look after her parents. I'll see you soon." Karen hung up and shifted in her seat to face Summer. She stroked the girl's hair. "Summer. Summer, wake up."

Zac jerked on the other sofa and sat bolt upright as soon as he heard Karen's voice, rubbing his eyes and yawning.

Summer stirred, her eyes flickering upon hearing a voice.

"They've found Lottie. She's okay," Karen said in a calm tone.

Zac looked up at the ceiling and blew out his cheeks, feeling the same relief Karen had experienced moments ago.

"She's okay?" Summer replied, her voice croaky.

"Yes, darling. She's safe and unharmed. Police officers are taking her home right now. Jade and Belinda are there to make sure she arrives safely. You can see her tomorrow once we've spoken to her."

Summer offered a weak smile at Karen and then towards her dad, as a tear fell from the corner of her eye.

Zac rose from the sofa. "How about we get you to bed? I can sleep on the floor beside you in case you need me."

Summer nodded as she rose and scooped up her phone and hoodie. She kissed Karen on the cheek, Karen responding with a hug. Zac looked on before reaching out to squeeze Karen's hand. He mouthed, *thank you*. "Don't head home tonight. It's too late. You need to sleep as well.

See you in the morning," he said, kissing Karen good night.

## 39

Though Karen craved a good night's sleep, she had tossed and turned through the night, her mind too wired to settle. She'd spiralled through moments of bizarre dreams or staring wide-eyed at the dark ceiling above her, to getting out of bed and padding across the hallway to Summer's room and staring at Summer through the open doorway. So many thoughts had crossed her mind as she'd stared at the girl she had grown so fond of. Never in her wildest dreams had she imagined herself in this situation with a man she loved, albeit now sleeping on the floor in his daughter's room, his snores vibrating through the carpet, and his daughter who now had a better relationship with Karen than she did with her own mum.

She had left them both sleeping in this morning, with Zac choosing to take a few days of annual leave to be with his daughter. As she swiped through the internal doors to her block, her legs felt like heavy sacks of concrete as she trudged along the corridor. Her mind felt frazzled, her body ached, and confusion clouded her judgement. Pushing through the door to her office, she placed her bag on the visitor's chair and took off her jacket before hanging it on the coat stand. Stepping over to her window, she opened it, needing the fresh air to blow away the staleness which lingered in the room.

Karen headed to the main SCU floor after making herself a cup of strong black coffee. The team was short in numbers today. Many had worked past their shift last night in the search for Lottie Traynor, with officers being pulled in from the TSG, traffic, and the robbery, trafficking, and sexual crime teams from CID. Even her least favourite DCI, DCI Carl Shield, had released all available officers from his team to help. It was a well-coordinated effort across the entire police force which had led to a safe and happy conclusion.

Claire, Ned, and Preet were the main officers in from her team. Karen walked over to Claire's desk and grabbed a free chair before wheeling it beside Claire's.

"What a night," Karen said, blowing across the top of her mug.

"It sounded pretty intense, but I'm glad Lottie's home," Claire said. "How is the DCI's daughter? A traumatic experience for her as well."

"Shaken up and shocked. It will take some time to process it. Zac has taken a few days off to be with her. It's half-term next week, so he's going to square it up with the school for her to start her break earlier."

"That's good," Preet said, listening in. "Do you think it was a random abduction?"

Karen took a sip of her coffee and winced as the scorching liquid singed her tongue.

"I don't know. It's something I've dealt with on a few occasions in London, but the victims have often been older. I've seen Eastern European OCGs abduct young women off the streets and hold them against their will in illegal brothels. They'll drug them up and shift them between hotels, B & Bs, and rented accommodation selling their bodies for sex. Bloody nightmare trying to rescue girls in that situation because their locations change daily, so intel is always out of date within hours."

"I can't imagine it being the case with Lottie. After all, they released her a few hours later," Preet said.

"True. Perhaps they realised how young she was and needed to dump her. Underage prostitution is something completely different. It carries stiffer sentences if caught and is more often found in secretive paedo rings hiding on the Dark Web selling live images of underage girls being sexually abused to pay-per-view customers across the world."

Karen had witnessed the after-effects of such low life depravity while uncovering a global paedo ring. With cooperation from the UK Child Exploitation and Online Protection Centre, the FBI in the US, Dutch police, Thai police, and her colleagues in Essex, Liverpool, and Glasgow, they had smashed an international paedo ring spanning over thirty countries. The investigation had rescued over two hundred children from abuse and arrested a hundred and seventy suspects, and the discovery of over sixty thousand members in the heavily encrypted forum.

"So why take her? Mistaken identity?" Claire speculated.

"Could be. We'll know more once Lottie has been interviewed a few times. It will be a slow and painstaking process to draw the information out of her. It's not something we can rush. Too many questions and forcing her to relive the experience may cause her to shut down. Not deliberately," Karen pointed out for clarity, "but a subconscious mechanism by her mind to protect her from the painful flashbacks and the feelings associated with the experience. It's the brain's natural self-defence mechanism."

"The suspects could disappear before we have clear descriptions of them," Claire pointed out.

Karen nodded. "I know. There's a fine balance between protecting the victim and gathering the evidence in time to act upon it.

"Our focus still needs to be on tracking down Dale Cready. We can now place him at the murder scene of William Armstrong and, with his MO, we can assume he was also responsible for Michael's murder," Karen said. Her phone pinged on the desk in front of her. Karen put her mug down and checked the screen. It wasn't a caller registered in her contacts list, but the message was clear.

Robert Bagshaw wanted to meet.

## 40

As KAREN STOOD OUTSIDE, she scanned the street. Robert Bagshaw's instructions had been explicit. Karen was to meet him in a public place, and he'd chosen Costa Coffee within the Premier Inn on Blossom Street. Busy in her opinion, with a comfortable flow of pedestrians heading in and out of town. Traffic rumbled at a snail's pace as vehicles slowed for the traffic lights. She nodded approvingly. Next door to the Premier Inn was the Windmill pub with a council-run CCTV camera in front of it, its lens pointing back in the direction of the Premier Inn. There were further cameras fixed to buildings next to Micklegate Bar, one of the historic $14^{th}$ century medieval main stone gateways to the city for anyone arriving from the south. *He chose this spot well*, Karen thought.

Karen headed into the coffee shop and glanced round, not spotting Robert Bagshaw to begin with. Although Karen had seen his pictures on the system, she wasn't prepared for how different he looked in person. She found him tucked away in a corner, his hands cradling a coffee. His eyes widened, and he shifted in his seat as Karen approached.

Pulling out her warrant card, Karen held it out in front of her to allay Bagshaw's fears. "Robert, Detective Chief Inspector Karen Heath," she said, sliding into the seat opposite him. "You're a hard man to track down."

Bagshaw smiled weakly, his lips hardly moving. "There's nothing else I can do. I need to keep moving. Last night, I stayed upstairs," Bagshaw said, gesturing towards the Premier Inn reception desk.

"I know you're scared. We are doing everything we can to protect you and your family. Your wife and daughter are safe. That's the main thing. I need to take you to them. That way we can look after all three of you."

Bagshaw shook his head. He licked his lips as his eyes scanned the sea of faces scattered round the coffee shop. "You don't get it do you? You can't stop these people. They are dangerous and unforgiving. I swear, I didn't know anything about this. I'm an accountant. Just a bloody accountant. Lee Harman employed me to be one of two accountants. I thought William and I were both working on the business together. But soon we found out that Lee Harman had assigned William to work on a different business, Denby Construction. I didn't know what was going on," Bagshaw said, his voice strained and desperate.

"I know. You're an innocent victim in all of this, but you have the information we need to bring this to an end. Have you got the envelope with you?" Karen asked.

Bagshaw nodded, reaching into his jacket and pulling out a small envelope. He slid it across the table before grabbing his coffee and taking a sip.

Karen glanced over her shoulder to make sure no one was watching before she handled the envelope. Inside was one sheet of A4 paper with "*#282467*" written by hand. She stared at the information and narrowed her eyes, perplexed as to its meaning.

"Do you know what this means?" she asked.

Bagshaw shook his head. "Not a clue. It's got nothing to do with me."

"It could be a reference number? An access code? A password?" Karen suggested, hoping it might jolt his memory.

Bagshaw shrugged.

Karen replaced the letter in the envelope and dropped it into a clear evidence bag before pulling out her phone. "I've got officers standing by. This is what you're going to do. They will pull up outside Costa. You and I will leave here in one car, and we'll take you to see your wife and daughter. Then, we will need to interview you formally for the record. You need to give us your side of the story. Are you happy with that?"

Bagshaw shrugged. "I'm not happy with any of it. None of this. I want my life back."

"You will get it back. There are a few things we need to do first. Are you ready?"

Bagshaw drained the last of his coffee and nodded. Karen put in the call. A few minutes later, four plain-clothed officers, two of which were AFOs, concealing their weapons inside their jackets, met Karen and Bagshaw at the entrance to the coffee shop. As the officers closed in on Bagshaw, Karen made sure he was secure and escorted him to two unmarked cars with engines still running.

Karen hopped into the back of one of them with Bagshaw.

Karen glanced across to Bagshaw, who looked terrified. As he checked his surroundings, his eyes were as jumpy as his body. Karen gave the officers the order to move as her phone rang in her hand. Glancing at the screen, she didn't recognise the number but took the call anyway.

"Take yesterday as a warning. We've shown you how easy it is to hurt those round you. Back off because you don't know who you're dealing with," the muffled Irish voice hissed. "Yesterday it was Lottie. Next time it could be Summer. We can hurt you in so many ways that you'll hate yourself for the rest of your life. You don't want your nearest and dearest to end up dead, stuffed inside a suitcase, and chucked into the river, do you? Do the right thing."

An icy chill slithered down Karen's spine as the caller hung up. Her breath caught in her throat as her stomach churned and a wave of nausea washed over her. *Shit.*

## 41

Waves of panic turned to flashes of anger as Karen returned to the station while Bagshaw went to the hotel with armed officers. Karen paced round the grounds calming the tide of rage that charged through her veins. Karen's investigation had resulted in Lottie's abduction. The Harmans were behind this, which only infuriated her further.

She dialled Zac's number. He answered a few moments later.

"Hey, you. Sorry I wasn't awake when you left this morning."

"That's fine. You both needed to rest. Listen, I've had an anonymous call. I think the Harmans were behind Lottie's abduction as a way of scaring me off."

"What?" Zac said.

"Yes. The caller said they could get to me anytime or anywhere and hurt those closest to me. He said it was

Lottie this time, but it could be Summer next if I don't back off." Karen listened as Zac's breathing intensified, knowing he was angry. "I need you to make sure you're both extra vigilant. Don't let Summer out of your sight for the next few days. I'll arrange for extra officers to be positioned on rota outside and get a panic button installed linked to the control room."

"I think I can look after Summer," Zac replied curtly.

She shut her eyes as the silence enveloped them both.

"Sorry. I shouldn't have snapped at you like that. I'm just really mad and tired right now."

Swallowing hard, she nodded, hating the awkwardness between them. "I know. I'm mad too. We need to keep this from Summer. Tell her you're going to have lots of movies and pizza days with her. The mention of both will excite her."

"Yes. I guess. Keep in touch and let me know what's happening," Zac said, his voice deflated by now as he hung up.

Karen trudged back into her building with an overbearing wave of guilt washing over her.

The unit buzzed with the arrival of more members of her team. Karen went to the front of the room and told her officers about the anonymous phone call. Many shook their heads in annoyance, while others muttered obscenities under their breath.

"Such threats will not put us off. It only makes me more determined than ever to bring them all down." Karen pulled the envelope from the evidence bag. Turning to the whiteboard, she grabbed a marker and copied the code from the paper. Stepping back, she turned to her officers. "This was the only thing William left Bagshaw. I don't know what it is? Any thoughts?"

"It's not a grid reference, so we can rule out a location," Ed said.

"Password?" another suggested.

"Possibly," Karen replied. "We are in trouble if it's for a website," Karen said. Her team stayed deep in thought, crunching through as many ideas as possible with suggestions being thrown from all sides of the room. Karen chipped in with her own ideas. "I thought it looked like an entry code for a building. An office maybe? But that might be anywhere, and not even in York." The more she thought about it, the more impossible it felt to find the meaning of the code.

"William told Bagshaw he had important information stored away for safekeeping. What could that mean?" Karen said, extending her hands out in front of her. "Stored away for *safe* keeping. A vault? Secure garage? Perhaps a bank or a PO box? It has to be a folder, a USB stick, document, or photographic evidence." Karen was spitballing but hoped the collective brainstorming would help.

"Were any keys recovered from the Armstrongs' property suitable for a safe deposit box in a bank?" Ty asked.

The exhibits officer attached to Karen's team checked the logs. "Several house and door keys. A shed key. And eight keys suitable for padlocks, though only three locks were recovered from the property. It's not unusual for people to accumulate a mass of keys through time. Keys belonging to a safe deposit box have three or four digits printed on them," the officer replied, nodding towards the whiteboard.

Karen paused for thought as she walked round the desks. "I guess the same would apply for a PO box?"

The exhibits officer nodded. "They would have a small reference number punched into the key."

Claire chipped in next. "There are PO boxes at Micklegate and York post offices. I don't know about the one at Micklegate, but York post office charges three hundred to four hundred pounds a year to rent one, and there have been no annual payments to the post office from William's bank accounts for the last few years."

"That's good to know," Karen replied. "For the time being, let's keep thinking about this code. The more ideas we have the better. One other thing, start checking all the hotels and B & Bs in York. Call or visit them. We are looking for anyone who has checked in recently matching Dale Cready's description. If you hit a brick wall, then extend your search to outside of the city centre. We need to find him. He is lying low somewhere. Where?"

Karen left the team to spend the rest of the afternoon working on those key action points while she went and updated the super.

## 42

KAREN PARKED her car at the Big Yellow storage site. Every available officer not needing to be desk-bound had spent the rest of yesterday afternoon and all evening making dozens of enquiries at PO box locations, post offices, and storage units across the city. Three self-storage sites had confirmed their entry keypads needed a combination of digits and symbols to allow owners access. Officers had checked all three using the code found in William's envelope. Officers had ruled out two sites, but they'd found the code in William's envelope worked on the entry keypad at the Big Yellow storage site, which allowed the big glass doors to slide open.

Excited by the breakthrough, Karen met Jade and Ed at the entrance. "Morning, you two. Have you been in?"

With a light drizzle overnight, the temperature had dropped a few degrees this morning. Though the weather was mild, Karen sensed a change in the air. The country had clung on to the last remnants of summer ,but couldn't hold back the slide into autumn where the evenings closed in quicker, and on some days a hoodie was needed to stay warm indoors. It's also the time when meals turned from light snacks and salads to hearty, warm and comforting foods.

"Not yet." Jade said. "We were waiting for you and used the time to talk to the site manager. He checked his records and found no evidence of William Armstrong or David Cooper in their system. I even tried Jean Armstrong and Mary Cooper in case William had set up an account in her name. Nothing there either."

"I showed the four remaining padlock keys recovered from the Armstrongs' property," Ed said, holding up the clear evidence bag. "He believes that one of them is a standard-issue Big Yellow storage padlock key. Every person renting a unit has to take one as part of the contract. They have a small bank of tiny storage compartments towards the rear of the first floor. They're the cheapest and smallest, so seems a good place to start?"

Karen glanced up to see CCTV footage overlooking the main entrance where the keypad and sliding doors were situated. Without knowing when and if William had last visited, Karen couldn't afford to devote the resources to scanning their video archives. "Right. Shall we take a look?"

Jade punched in the code again, and the large sliding doors opened. The drop in temperature was notable as Karen shivered. Large steel fabricated buildings felt like saunas during the summer and iceboxes during the winter. A few people milled about, loading or unloading stock from the larger units on the ground floor. One particular open unit had a door the size of a garage door. Two men were inside loading stock on to a pallet truck from shelves of sweets and chocolates. Karen's eyes widened. *Heaven for someone with a sweet tooth*, she thought.

After taking the elevator to the first floor, they followed the instructions provided to them by the staff. They passed nondescript bland grey corridors lined with identical steel walls and bright yellow doors, each one locked with a standard-issue Big Yellow storage padlock. They walked to the end of one corridor and found a low-level steel box containing dozens of doors only six inches wide and a few inches high, each one locked with a padlock.

"Can't fit much in these, not even a packed lunch," Jade remarked.

Jade was right. Karen imagined these were used to store files or paperwork people didn't want stored at home in case of a burglary or fire.

"Try the keys, Ed. You take two and I'll take two," Jade said.

Ed and Jade snapped on latex gloves before trying the keys in each of the locks. It took a few minutes before a lock snapped open and Ed stepped back open-mouthed. He glanced at Karen, who looked just as surprised as she raised a brow. She nodded for him to go ahead. Removing the padlock and opening a small door, Ed peered in and pulled out a bank card, USB stick, and a folded sheet of paper.

"It's a bank card in the name of Bill Carnforth," Ed said, handing the card to Jade.

"And here's a bank statement in the same name with a one hundred and forty grand balance, and one prepayment for the storage unit of ten grand," he added, handing that to Jade as well.

"No wonder they didn't have any record of him. He used false details," Karen said. "Right, put the lock back on and let's head back to the office."

---

THE NEWS of the discovery injected a fresh wave of enthusiasm into the team. They had discovered the missing money Dale Cready was looking for, which put Cready in a helpless position, though he didn't know that yet.

With her team assembled towards the front of the office and all eyes fixed on the big monitor, Karen plugged the USB stick into the connected laptop. There were dozens of folders containing documents, while others held MP3 audio files. Karen clicked through a few of the folders and paused when she discovered a copy of a hidden ledger of cash transactions being moved round Paul Harman's business. The author of the ledger was William Armstrong. Karen realised William had created backup copies as an insurance policy, one which had cost him his life.

Karen clicked on a PDF document and sucked in a sharp intake of breath. "Look at this," Karen said, scanning the details. "A copy of a bank statement in Lee Harman's name. The bank is in Jersey, and it received regular deposits from that ledger to the sum of seven hundred and fifty thousand pounds, with no withdrawals."

"Cunning sod," an officer said. "No capital gains tax, transfer tax, VAT, withholding tax or wealth tax. It's a very tax efficient way of hiding your money."

"Yes, through my legal training I learned that Jersey is a hotspot for corporate fraud, bribery and corruption, insider dealing, and market abuse," Ed added.

"Well, we can bring this to the attention of the financial regulators in both the UK and Jersey and the financial crime unit," Karen said. The more she examined the files the more she uncovered. The Harmans had hidden most of their criminal activity behind legal entities, and in running two separate financial accounting structures and several shell companies abroad, could siphon off large sums of money and avoid paying tax, with much of the paperwork signed off by both Paul and Lee Harman. They had defrauded financial backers, liquidated companies and silenced dissenters through bribery, blackmail, and violence.

Sifting through the files revealed a series of audio recordings William had secretly recorded. Many involved Paul talking to others on the phone about the illegal movement of money to reduce their tax liability while also keeping Jersey topped up. Karen could only assume Jersey was a reference to Lee's bank account though none of the recordings mentioned Lee's name directly.

Karen stood back and scanned the evidence. She breathed a sigh of relief. There was enough there to keep Paul Harman in prison and bring criminal proceedings against Lee Harman. With evidence from Robert Bagshaw and Councillor Kumar, the screw was tightening on the Harman Empire.

## 43

Karen headed to see the detective superintendent with the exciting news and bumped into Kelly as she left a meeting room.

"Ah, ma'am, I was coming to see you. Are you busy?"

"No. I've got an hour or two before my next meeting, so let's head back to my office."

Karen followed in silence, a step behind her boss. It was one of those awkward relationships where face-to-face meetings across a desk would be fine, but they had little to say to each other while walking along. She couldn't blurt out, "so how's your day going?" or "how was your evening. Did you get up to anything good?" She could do that with DI Anita Mani, who she had grown fond of. She was easy to talk to, enjoyed a laugh, and was down to earth. Kelly was none of those things. Perhaps it was because of hierarchy and the need for Kelly to keep a professional distance between herself and officers of a lower rank. Whatever it was, Karen always found her boss hard to read.

Kelly opened the door to her office and went round to her side of the desk, placing her folders down and taking a seat. "I'm all ears."

"We've discovered the money William Armstrong had hidden, along with a memory stick containing incriminating information on the Harmans, including evidence of money being siphoned off to an offshore account in Jersey."

Kelly sat back, raising a brow. "Brilliant. That's great news. Well done."

Karen smiled. "Thank you, ma'am."

Karen took a few moments to update Kelly on the contents of the stick, including bank statements, audio recordings of Paul Harman, and a network of shell companies.

"I'll be handing the evidence over to the tax authorities, financial crime unit, and the regulatory authorities in both countries. First, I need to locate and arrest Cready for the double homicide. With your permission, I'd like to set a trap and use Bagshaw as bait."

Kelly considered the request. "What resources do you need?"

"My officers, a couple of uniforms, and a team of AFOs. Cready has a marker for firearms. I'm not prepared to take any risks and put Bagshaw or my officers in danger."

Kelly rested her elbows on her armrests and formed a steeple with her fingers as she considered the situation. "Do it."

"Thanks, ma'am," Karen said, rising from her chair and heading back to her unit.

An hour later, Karen and Jade parked at the hotel and made their way up to the first floor and room 112. They had chosen the room for several reasons. Taking a ground-floor bedroom would have left the Bagshaws vulnerable to attack through a window. A room higher than the first floor would have made an emergency escape time-consuming.

Room 112 was being guarded by a plain-clothes firearms officer, while another AFO was stationed by the fire exit, with a clear view of the entire corridor leading to the elevators. Karen presented her card to the first officer, who nodded before knocking on her behalf. Bagshaw opened the door a few inches and peered through the gap, and upon seeing Karen opened the door and stood aside to allow Karen and Jade to enter.

The suite comprised a lounge area, a large bedroom, and a kitchenette. Elizabeth and Chloe were sitting on the sofa watching TV. Crease lines appeared on Elizabeth's face, the strain taking its toll on her. Karen offered her a reassuring smile before turning to Robert Bagshaw.

"Can we talk in private away from your daughter?" Karen said, nodding towards the bedroom.

Bagshaw padded into the bedroom, followed by his wife, Elizabeth, Karen, and Jade, who shut the door behind them. Bagshaw paced round the room, while Elizabeth perched on the end of the bed. Clothes lay scattered on the bed, a small supply of toiletries sat on a side cupboard, and a stale smell lingered in the air.

"How much longer have we got to stay here?" Bagshaw moaned.

"We're getting closer. We've discovered information that William had stored away. It's enough to bring the Harmans down for good. But there's something else," Karen said, throwing a quick glance in Jade's direction, who stood beside the window, peering out over the car park looking for signs of Cready.

Bagshaw stuffed his hands in his pockets and pulled his arms in close to his body.

"We want to set a trap for Cready, so we'd like to take you back to the house you're renting. We need to get you out in the open and catch him when he comes to find you."

Bagshaw glanced at his wife and then shook his head. "No. Absolutely no. Are you bloody crazy? Are you trying to get me killed?" he shouted.

Elizabeth chewed on her bottom lip and stared at her husband.

Karen was expecting that reaction, so let the thought settle with him first before she continued.

"Dale Cready is after the envelope and the code. We have those in our possession. There is nothing he can do. We want to set up an operation monitoring both of the properties you're renting. He's out to find you, so I'm certain he'll visit both places. We can only catch him if we mount an operation."

Bagshaw backed away. "You are crazy. You want to use me as bait and don't care what happens to me?"

Karen shook her head. "It's not like that at all. We are not leaving you alone. Both properties will be under constant surveillance with officers inside and out. We grab him the minute we see him. I promise you will not be alone for one second." Karen softened her voice. "Your safety is my key priority. I want to put these evil people behind bars so they can never hurt you or your family again. We can talk about your plans for the future once this is all over. You could start a new life here or in another country."

Bagshaw closed his eyes as his shoulders heaved.

"It's the only way we can bring this to a conclusion. Even though we'll have officers stationed at the bungalow and the caravan park, we want to have you at the bungalow to start with."

Bagshaw opened his eyes and stared at Elizabeth who sighed heavily and nodded before looking down at her feet. It took a few moments before he nodded. "Okay."

## 44

BACK AT THE BASE, over thirty officers crammed into a conference room. A large contingent from Karen's team formed the majority, along with six AFOs, two dog handlers and several uniformed colleagues. It was a large operation in Karen's mind, and the safety of her officers was as key to her as protecting Robert Bagshaw.

Karen took her position at the front of the room. "Thank you for coming. I'll keep this brief. I have given you a pack. Within it are pictures of Dale "Tin Snips" Cready, a dangerous enforcer from Manchester with a marker for firearms. He is our prime suspect in the double homicide of two brothers, Michael and William Armstrong. I've also included site maps for the two locations we'll cover in our operation." Karen paused for a moment, allowing the officers to flick through the various pages. "We believe Cready is looking for Robert Bagshaw and will visit one, if not both properties rented in Bagshaw's name. I need him apprehended alive and with minimal risk to the public."

Karen nodded in Jade's direction, who stood and came over to join Karen.

"I'll be leading the surveillance operation at the caravan park," Jade began. "The DCI will be in charge of the second team at the bungalow. The team sheet in the pack will confirm which team you've been assigned to, and we will have officers stationed within both properties and outside. There will be a dog unit at both locations, along with a team of firearms officers."

"Thanks, Jade." Karen scanned the sea of eager faces. "As soon as we get eyes on Cready, it will be up to the firearms officers to move in first. They need to secure him under control before any other officers move in, understood?"

The officers nodded, with a few exchanging hushed conversations as they discussed the operation.

"Do we know a rough location for Cready?" an officer asked from the middle of the crowd.

"I'm afraid not. My team has been running checks with all the local hotels, B & Bs, and guest houses. No one matching Cready's description is among their guests. He could be lying low in a car or using his contacts to hide him."

"He might travel in from somewhere else?" another officer suggested.

Karen agreed. Cready could be miles away and using a vehicle to move round the city. "It's assumed he's been using a car and there have been multiple vehicle thefts recently. ANPR alerts have been set up for all of them. There have been three further reported car thefts in the York area during the last few hours. We have circulated the registration details and descriptions of all these vehicles too, and they are in the back of your packs."

"What's the likelihood of him showing up tonight?" an AFO asked.

"In all honesty, I don't know. He'll be getting desperate. Time is money. Robert Bagshaw is his only lead to finding the stolen money, but we have located it and requested a freeze on the account. So Cready couldn't access it even if he wanted to. He's looking for Bagshaw, and the most likely places to find him are at the properties rented in his name."

"Cready might not appear today, tomorrow or even next week?" the AFO added.

Karen paced up and down in front of the officers, sensing the frustration in the officer's voice. "He'll show up in the next day or two. He is losing money the longer he is stuck on this job. He's methodical and dangerous, but I'm expecting him to slip up. Any questions?"

With silence in the room and many officers getting jumpy in their seats and keen to get on with the job, Karen dismissed the team and headed back to her office to get ready for this evening.

## 45

WITH SUNSET COME AND GONE, dark shadows spread across the pavement like ghostly tendrils. The nights always brought a more sinister feel to the streets with fewer cars, even fewer pedestrians, and the hustle, bustle, and noise of the day petering out to nothing more than the occasional boy racer with a loud exhaust puncturing the silence, or the cry of a fox.

Karen had earlier organised officers to do several sweeps of the street acting as takeaway delivery drivers on mopeds in case Cready or Harman's henchmen were staking out the place.

With the location being given the all-clear, Karen had parked beneath a tree, its branches casting dark shadows across her windscreen and providing a natural camouflage to those walking by. She'd positioned a white transit van across the street to Bagshaw's rented bungalow. Inside were two firearms officers and three of Karen's detectives. Further up the road was a grey Mondeo estate dog unit. Bagshaw sat in the lounge, accompanied by a firearms officer and two more of Karen's team. A uniformed officer stood by a bedroom window at the rear of the property.

With everyone in position, it was now a waiting game.

Surveillance operations were anything other than glamorous. Television dramas and movies turned what was often a dull, cold, and tiring task into something more swashbuckling and exciting.

"Do you think we'll get lucky tonight?" Ed asked, sitting in the passenger seat of Karen's car.

Karen opened her flask of coffee and poured two cups, handing one to Ed. "I hope so. The net is closing in on Cready. He's also running out of victims to target to get the information he needs." Karen sipped her black coffee and savoured the warmth as it raced down her throat and warmed her belly.

"The team were having bets about who would get lucky. Our team or the DS's," Ed laughed.

"How is it looking for us?"

"Of course, everyone said we would. You scare them to vote otherwise," he teased.

The conversation flowed back and forth between them for the next few hours. It was a good way to stay awake as the clock closed in on midnight. Ed was an easy person to get on with, and Karen enjoyed listening to his opinions on everything, which were both intellectual and heartfelt. Yes, he dressed impeccably and wouldn't look out of place sitting at the front of a court, but there were no airs and graces with Ed. He wasn't flash, flamboyant, or cocky like Ty. They were complete opposites, and Karen was sure Ed had a long and successful career ahead of him in the police, as he'd spoken about his wish to become at least a DI.

Karen picked up her two-way comms and spent the next few minutes checking in with her team. So far, all was quiet in and round the bungalow. Reaching for her phone, Karen dialled Jade's number and waited a few seconds before Jade answered. "Anything to report?"

"No, nothing here, Karen. Quite a few of the caravans are empty. I guess most of these are holiday homes. But there are a few permanent residents dotted in and round the park, but situated towards the main entrance where the shops are as well. This part of the park is much quieter, which helps us. If he turns up here there's less risk to the public."

"How's Belinda?" Karen asked, knowing she was sharing the car with Jade.

"Doesn't stop bloody talking."

Jade's comment had Belinda protesting her innocence, which made Karen laugh as she listened to the exchange at the other end of the line.

"Okay, I'll touch base with you again in a few hours." Karen hung up and placed her phone on the dashboard.

The hours dragged on. The lack of movement had left most officers with tired eyes, sore bums, stiff hips, and numb legs. It was nearly three a.m. when Karen's radio crackled into life. She jumped in her seat.

"Movement at the rear of the adjacent property. It might just be a fox, but I can hear rustling in the bushes at the end of the garden," her officer said, whispering through the comms.

Karen's heartbeat quickened; her body was desperate to leap from the car. She hung on every word, briefly glancing across to Ed who seemed as wired and ready to fling open his door and run towards the bungalow.

"Everybody stand by," Karen instructed.

"Still can't see anything," the officer continued. "Movement has stopped."

Karen blew out her cheeks and felt deflated.

A minute later the officer was back with another update. "Movement again in the neighbouring garden. Stand by. I can confirm we have a suspect in the neighbouring garden." A small gap in the clouds for a few brief seconds allowed the moon to cast its natural light across the gardens. "Dark clothing and... ski mask. They are carrying a holdall. Making their way up the garden. Stand by."

Tension rippled through Karen's body, the hair on the back of her neck standing on end as a surge of adrenaline coursed through her veins. Every muscle in her body felt like a coiled spring ready to be released. Ed swallowed hard, one hand leaning against the door, the other on the handle in readiness. Every officer waited for a further update.

"Stand by. Suspect has climbed over the fence and is now at the rear of our property. He is at the rear door to the kitchen."

Karen pressed the button on her comms to reach the officers in the white van and the dog unit. "Kilo One and Kilo Two make a silent approach to the front of the property." Karen exited her vehicle with Ed and met up with her other officers. The two AFOs took the lead and approached the front door, with everyone else lined up behind them.

"Suspect is trying the kitchen door. Stand by," the officer inside whispered. "Suspect has entered the property."

"Go, go, go!" Karen said into her comms.

The shouts and screams from the AFOs broke the silence of the night as they charged through the front door. "Armed police! Stay where you are! Get on the floor now!" Their colleague from the lounge kept the door shut to protect Bagshaw, who cowered on the sofa, his arms over his head, his body trembling. Torches fixed to the top of their MP5 submachine guns shone beams of light round the darkened kitchen and outlined the silhouette of the suspect dressed in black jeans, black hoodie, black rubber gloves, and a black ski mask. A navy holdall lay beside him.

They outnumbered the suspect with three AFOs training their weapons on him while Karen's detectives cuffed him from behind and put him in the seated position.

Karen snapped on a pair of latex gloves before removing the ski mask. She groaned and looked up at Ed with a shake of her head. The suspect they had apprehended was a white male, not Cready.

"Shit," Karen muttered, getting to her feet. "What's your name?"

The man remained silent, staring at the floor.

One of her officers put on a pair of gloves before pulling back the zip on the navy holdall. "We've got a hammer, several screwdrivers, another pair of gloves, and what looks like the proceeds from other burglaries carried out in the area. A laptop, iPad, items of jewellery, cash, and a watch."

Karen groaned as she stepped back with a heavy sigh and a shake of her head. "Okay, thanks. Arrange transport for him to be taken back to the nick. Charge him with breaking and entering."

Karen stepped out into the hallway and through the front door. The commotion had stirred the neighbourhood. Neighbours wrapped in dressing gowns stood in their gardens with panicked looks, while others peered through the safety of their bedroom windows. If Cready was about and watching, they had missed their opportunity. She would stand down her officers and call it a night.

## 46

BLEARY EYES and tired faces greeted Karen in the station canteen as she grabbed a coffee and two slices of toast, before joining Jade at the table with a few other officers.

"I feel like death today," Jade said, groaning before burying her head into her arms on the table. "Wake me up next week."

Karen didn't want to eat but needed the energy. She slathered her toast with lots of butter and marmalade before taking a bite and welcoming the sweetness. There was something very comforting about marmalade on toast. Perhaps it was because her dad had insisted on Mum's home-made marmalade at the breakfast table when she was growing up. She'd tried it as a child and hadn't warmed to it, not enjoying the bitterness of the chunky orange rind. She had reconnected with it, having spent the start of so many shifts in greasy spoon cafés while in uniform, the habit continuing when she joined CID.

It amazed her how something so trivial as the taste of marmalade could reinvoke so many childhood memories which had laid dormant deep within her mind. She smiled, remembering the contented look on her dad's face as he'd nodded approvingly at her mum.

She swallowed down the mouthful with a glug of coffee. "Well, that didn't go as I had planned."

Jade lifted her tired head, her lids drooping. "Well, we still got a result of sorts. The bloke we arrested last night was Ian Welch, a prolific burglar. The burglary and robbery squad have been after him for months and they're fuming that we stumbled upon him and got the collar." Jade offered a weak smile and wink. "He's suspected of committing nineteen burglaries in the area over the last twelve months. The authorities released him only fifteen months ago after he had served three years out of a six-year sentence."

Karen raised a brow. "Good for them. That will boost their clear-up rates, thanks to us."

No one wanted to talk as they ate in silence and ordered more coffee, waiting for the caffeine to kick in.

After finishing, Karen and Jade headed back to the SCU. They were thin on the ground today, with the officers who'd helped on the op last night told to come in after lunch as they'd be repeating the op again this evening.

Karen checked the whiteboard and shouted, "Anything to report that hasn't been added to the board?"

"We've been going through the evidence on the memory stick," Dan said. "It's thrown up more evidence of a line of financial transactions to Spain and then on to Peru."

"Have we traced the account holder's details yet?" Karen asked, taking a detour to Dan's desk.

"On my list to do next. It could be a route that the Harmans were using to bring drugs into the country?"

"If it was Peru, then yes. See what else you can find," Karen instructed.

Ned approached. "Karen, someone called our control room yesterday and reported that they found a white male beaten and semi-conscious. Control dispatched officers to the scene and the victim was taken to the hospital yesterday morning. His fingers were broken on his right hand with a partial separation of his little pinky finger."

Karen gasped as she narrowed her eyes. "Why weren't we told about this earlier?"

Ned shrugged. "They didn't think about contacting us."

Karen sighed. She hated it when there was a breakdown in communication. Part of the MO fitted Cready. "Jade, don't get too comfortable. We might have another potential victim."

## 47

KAREN PULLED OPEN the door to the ward and tutted as she waited for Jade to apply liberal amounts of hand gel from the pump dispenser beside the door. "Finished?"

Jade rolled her eyes. "You can never get enough hand gel. I don't want to be catching sepsis."

"Jade, we are visiting a ward, not a highly infectious and plague-ridden place, where we need to wear military NBC suits to go in."

Karen asked at the nurses' desk for Ciaran Ackley's bed. The nurse at the desk gave directions to the main ward which had eight beds, four on each side. Men of varying ages lay in their beds, a few closer to the end of their lives than others. Two old men lay beneath bed sheets, their bodies small, thin, and frail, their breath shallow and slow. Sadness washed over Karen as she walked by. She hated the thought of them lying there alone not surrounded by loved ones, with no one to talk to, no one to fuss over them, and feeling a sense of isolation and fear.

"Ciaran Ackley?" Karen said, finding the correct bed number.

His left eyelid and cheekbone were swollen as Ackley opened his eyes. He had a fat lip with crusty blood scabs, and red bruising to his jaw. They had bandaged his right hand. He nodded.

"Mr Ackley, I'm Detective Chief Inspector Karen Heath, and this is my colleague Detective Sergeant Jade Whiting. How are you feeling?"

"Okay," he replied, his swollen lips barely moving.

"We understand you suffered a serious injury to your hand. The nurses mentioned that you had undergone surgery yesterday to reattach your little finger. I know my uniformed colleagues took a statement from you, but I'd like to hear it from you in person. Can you give me a description of the person who attacked you?"

Ackley closed his eyes and looked away.

"Mr Ackley?"

"I can't think. It happened so quickly. I remember being approached and pulled to the ground from behind and being set upon."

Karen nodded. "Okay. Did your assailant say anything? Did he have an accent?"

Ackley shook his head.

"What about physical description? Was he short or tall? Stocky or thin? White or dark-skinned?"

"I can't remember. He appeared from nowhere in front of me and before I knew it, he had punched me in the face. I didn't have time to react or defend myself."

Jade, who stood round the other side of the bed looked at Karen, throwing her a confused look as she rubbed her tired eyes.

"I'm confused, Mr Ackley. You said he appeared from nowhere in front of you and then punched you, but a moment ago you said he pulled you to the ground from behind. Which was it?"

Ackley's lids flickered as he stared at the ceiling. "Behind, maybe the side. I can't remember. It happened so quickly. It's just a blur."

"And your attacker said *nothing*? You said in your first interview that nothing was stolen by the attacker, right? You still had your phone and wallet on you. That doesn't sound like a random robbery to me. It sounds like a targeted attack. Have you had any run-ins with people? Perhaps an argument?" Karen approached.

Ackley shook his head.

"So you don't know why this happened? Could they have been looking for information from you?"

Ackley fell silent, not looking at Karen or Jade, as Karen continued with her questioning.

"I understand you work for the council," Karen asked, changing tack. "In the finance department. I guess you get access to the names and addresses of most York residents?"

Ackley continued with this silence.

Karen pulled out her business card and left it in his bed. "Okay, Mr Ackley, I appreciate you don't want to talk now. Get some rest. If you think of anything or decide to talk to us, my number is on the card. We may know the individual responsible, but we need your help with a description."

Karen stepped out into the hospital corridor and waited again for Jade to drain the contents of the hand gel dispenser. "Try to save some for other visitors!" Karen said.

Jade ignored the jibe. "Cready's handiwork?"

"I think so." Karen mimicked a pair of scissors using her index and second finger. "Cready was disturbed, so he didn't complete the job. He targeted Ackley, to get the details of where Bagshaw might be."

Karen's phone rang as she walked towards the car, pressing a key fob to unlock the doors. "Dan, what's up?" she asked, opening her door and getting in as Jade came round to the passenger side.

"We've been alerted to a break-in this morning at a caravan at the Weir caravan park. It happened two hours ago, and CCTV footage caught the likely suspect prowling round the grounds. It was Cready. We just missed him."

Karen thumped the heel of her hand on the steering wheel. "Flipping hell. Give us a break. We missed him by a few hours. The fact he went there in daylight suggests he's getting desperate."

Karen hung up and relayed the information to Jade. "He'll target the house next. Hopefully tonight. Get in touch with the officers who are coming in this afternoon. Tell them to hold off until five p.m., briefing at six."

Jade nodded before getting on her phone and sending a text message to all involved.

The net was closing in on Cready. They had been so close to catching him.

## 48

Though she was shattered, going home to sleep seemed pointless with the briefing only a few hours away, so Karen headed over to Zac's for a shower and a change of clothes. Zac opened the door as Karen walked up the path.

"That's service for you," she said, arriving on the doorstep.

They stood awkwardly in the door for a moment, neither moving. Zac broke the silence first.

"Hey, listen. I'm sorry again for being so abrupt with you on the phone. I was out of order."

Karen batted away his apology, not wanting to make a fuss. "It's fine, seriously."

Zac reached out and held her hand. "No, it's not. You only had Summer's safety in mind when you told me about the anonymous call. I was pissed off and annoyed, and I took it out on you."

Karen smiled and leaned forward to kiss him. "Apology accepted."

"You looked shattered," Zac said, stepping to one side to let her in.

Karen dropped her handbag at the bottom of the stairs and hung her jacket on the newel post. "I am. I was on an op till four this morning. We were this close to catching Cready," Karen said, holding her thumb and index finger a centimetre apart. She updated Zac on how they had mounted a surveillance operation on both properties that Bagshaw was renting out.

"Coffee?" he offered, leading the way into the kitchen.

"Yes. And plenty of it. The stronger the better. I swear I have more coffee flowing through my veins than blood now." Karen took a seat at the dining table and ran a hand through her hair. It felt greasy and clumpy. "The good news is we caught a career criminal who has blighted York with a string of burglaries."

"So it wasn't all bad," Zac said, placing a coffee mug on a coaster in front of her.

Manky padded in and trotted over towards Karen, purring as he brushed his body round her ankles. She scooped him up in her arms and buried her face in his warm fur. "Ah, you missed me, baby boy." She smothered his fur with kisses before resting him on her lap and stroking his back. He curled into a ball and purred as he closed his eyes to snooze.

"Has he been okay?"

Zac took the chair opposite her and cupped a mug in his hands. "Good as gold. Sleeps all day, pops out to the garden to do a crap, comes back in and has a bite to eat, and goes back on to Summer's bed and falls asleep," he smiled.

"He's a good boy," she said, continuing to stroke him. "How is Summer?"

"I think she's okay. We went to see Lottie this morning which made her feel better. I gave Lottie and her family the space to come to terms with what they've been through. Summer has opened up a bit, and talking seems to have helped. I'll still offer her the chance to speak to a professional, so she bottles nothing up."

"Where is she?"

Zac nodded towards the ceiling; his brow raised. "Her bedroom. Netflix and Amazon Prime are getting serious usage from her."

Karen placed Manky on the floor and watched as he meandered off to his bed in the corner and buried himself deep in the blanket before falling asleep. "Is it okay if I see her? I need to grab a shower anyway."

"Sure. You don't have to ask. She'd love to see you."

Karen left half of her coffee, not being able to stomach any more.

Summer lay face down on her bed, her shoulders being propped up by two pillows as she watched a movie on her iPad with earbuds in her ears. Her legs were bent at the knees, her feet dancing in the air.

"Hey, Summer," Karen said, appearing in her doorway.

Summer looked up and pulled her earbuds away before sliding off the bed and coming over to give Karen a hug. The hug lasted longer than Karen expected as Summer rested her head on Karen's chest.

"Are you okay?" Karen asked.

Summer pulled away and smiled before flopping on to her bed again. "I'm good. Most of the time, anyway."

Karen perched on the end of the bed. "It will take time. You've got your Dad at home, and he is looking after you. I'm sorry I've not been round much, but work has been manic."

Summer shrugged. "That's okay. I know you're busy. It's just nice to see you."

"Ditto. I need to grab a shower and change of clothes. Back to work this evening. I know your Dad is here, but if there's anything you need you only have to call."

"I know." Summer plugged her earbuds back in and continued watching her movie.

Karen smiled. She admired the resilience of young people. They could bounce back so much quicker than adults. She had witnessed children endure the most horrific experiences and yet continued with their lives in ways that, if they had been adults, would have required years of therapy to regain any semblance of normality. Karen checked the time on her phone. A quick shower, change of clothes, and a bite to eat, in that order, before she'd scoot back to the office.

## 49

KAREN SLID down into her car seat and settled back while maintaining a visual on Bagshaw's bungalow in Rawcliffe. Having convened her team at six p.m. and spent fifteen minutes going through the briefing again, her officers set off in a convoy snaking through the streets before branching off to take up their positions. Karen didn't feel the need to have Bagshaw with them. Having discussed it with her team, if Cready came looking for Bagshaw, he would enter the property regardless, giving her officers plenty of time to apprehend him. Besides, Bagshaw had kicked up a stink and refused to be put in danger again after the events of last night, and she didn't blame him.

Fortunately for Karen she'd nabbed the same spot she had parked hours earlier. On this occasion, Jade accompanied her as she'd given Ed the night off. They'd parked the white transit opposite the bungalow. A dog unit had taken up position down the road, and two AFOs waited inside the property with two of Karen's officers.

She wasn't happy with Bagshaw being back at the hotel, but he needed to be with his family, so Karen had deployed extra officers to take up positions in the hotel car park, behind the main reception, and close to the fire exits.

Since both she and Jade were dressed in dark clothes, anyone walking past Karen's car would have to look twice to spot them, but it was unlikely they would see many people. The clouds were heavy, offering little to no chance of the moon poking through this evening. Karen spent the next few minutes checking in with everyone to make sure they were all set up and ready to go.

"Do you think he'll turn up tonight?" Jade asked, picking a crisp out of her packet and munching loudly on it.

Each crunch ground on Karen as she gritted her teeth. "Will you keep your mouth shut when you eat crisps? You remind me of a cow eating grass!"

Jade laughed as she shoved in a few more crisps and turned towards Karen, munching loudly.

"Jesus, it's like taking year threes out on a school trip," Karen said with a shake of her head.

"Well?"

"I'm hoping so. I don't think the super will allow more than another night or two of this."

"Hmm," Jade offered.

Karen's radio crackled into life twenty minutes later.

"Male turned into the road. Coming up behind my vehicle. Stand by," the dog handler said.

It was a tense few moments as Karen held her breath, her index finger tapping like mad against her thigh.

"It's a negative. The male is a Caucasian."

Karen let out an exasperated sigh. With a dry mouth and a tingling in her chest, she wished time would hurry up as fatigue and boredom crept in.

The hours ticked by. The odd car passed their vehicle, but other than the pedestrian they had seen earlier, the road was quiet. Jade took watch as much as she could, allowing Karen to doze. But there was too much on Karen's mind, which stopped her from falling into a deep sleep. It was what she would call, "I'm resting my eyes."

The whine of an approaching moped jolted her from her slumber. She blinked hard to shake the tiredness from her eyes as the noise grew louder. The moped whizzed past them and turned at the end of the road. A pizza delivery driver.

"Coffee?" Jade asked, leaning forward to retrieve the flask from between her legs.

"Good shout. I don't suppose you have any chocolate in your goody bag, do you?"

"I've got a Twirl. We can have half each?"

Karen yawned and blew out her cheeks. "I can live with that. I need a bit of sugar."

Jade unscrewed the lid from her flask and pulled out two paper cups from her bag, placing both of them on the dashboard. She was about to pour when the static from Karen's radio caused her to freeze.

"We have a male who has turned on to the road. Black clothing with his hoodie pulled low over his face. Stand by for more information."

Karen rubbed her clammy hands together as she clenched her jaw. Jade stuffed the cups back into her bag and replaced the lid on the flask, before placing her bag on the rear seat. They both lowered themselves further into their seats and remained motionless while watching the front of the house.

It felt like an eternity waiting for another update.

"Come on," Karen whispered.

"The male has passed me. He is not an IC1. I repeat, he is not an IC1. Possibly an IC2 or IC3. His hoodie made it difficult to confirm. He is tall and muscular with broad shoulders. Sticking close to the edge of the pavement and using the trees for cover. Coming your way," the officer said.

Karen reached for her radio. "Everybody stand by."

A few moments later, the man loomed into view. Karen and Jade slipped lower into their seats, barely able to look over the dashboard. They watched as the man slowed by Bagshaw's property, looked round, and then walked on.

"Do you think that's him?" Jade whispered.

"He fits the description. If it is him, then he's clever. He is doing a walk past to scope the scene and check for any sign of activity." Karen reached for her radio and had second thoughts before replacing it in her lap. "If it's him, he'll be back. He might try to gain access to the property from the rear."

A few minutes passed. Karen and her team were on tenterhooks, like tightly coiled springs in a box, ready to leap out. Officers were stationed at both ends of the street, so Karen would know within seconds if the individual left the area. They could stop the person for a routine police check.

"The individual has turned and is returning in your direction," an officer said over the radio.

Karen fidgeted in her seat. This was it. Call it instinct or gut feeling, but she was certain it was Cready. She watched as a dark shadow came back into view, the individual slowing the pace until they stopped on the pavement outside Bagshaw's property. He glanced round before slipping down the driveway towards the front door.

"Suspect is approaching the front door of the property," Karen whispered into her comms as she gripped her door handle. Jade doing the same.

"He's attempting to gain access," one of Karen's officers said from within the property.

Karen heard a faint crack as she saw the door open a few inches. Her heart raced as her muscles tensed and her skin prickled with anticipation.

She watched as the man slid through the open doorway and disappeared into the property. "Kilo One and Kilo Two, silent approach to the front of the property."

The side door to the white van slid open with two AFOs moving at speed towards the front of the bungalow, their approach silent. Karen's officers slipped in behind them. The dog handler covered the short distance, his panting dog straining at the leash.

Karen and Jade left her vehicle and as they crossed the road, it all kicked off.

"Armed police! Get down!" came voices from inside the property. "Get down now! Arms spread out to your sides," came further instructions.

Karen ran the short distance to the front of the property as extra firearms officers and the rest of her team ploughed through the front door.

Beams of white piercing light from torches fixed to MP5s and handheld torches lit up the darkened hallway. As Karen entered the property, she saw a man spreadeagled on the floor, the barrels of three MP5s inches away from his head. Specialist firearms officers were trained to aim for the head first to neutralise any threat. This change in policy had come about following jihadi knife attacks and suicide bombers in London and other major cities round the UK, which meant it was impossible for officers to get anywhere near to subdue them safely.

An officer knelt and pulled the hoodie back to identify the individual who was struggling to get loose from the officers pinning him to the floor. Close by lay a small black plastic bag. Inside was a pair of tin snips, a small length of rope, pliers, a large screwdriver, and a handgun.

One of the AFOs picked the handgun up by the grip and took it outside to inspect it.

"Is it real?" Karen asked, following behind the officer. She knew how real a replica could appear at first glance.

"Yes, ma'am. Glock 17 with ammunition."

"Shit," Karen mumbled as she headed back in.

Karen walked round a few of her officers to get a better look. She closed her eyes for a second and let out a sigh of relief as the weight of intimidation, threats and fear lifted. Dale Cready was finally in custody, ending her personal nightmare.

## 50

THE HULKING OUTLINE of Cready cut a cold and menacing figure as he sat as still as a waxwork figure across the table from Karen. Dressed in a white Tyvek suit, his clothes had been sent away for forensic analysis. They'd let him cool off in the cells for a few hours before placing him in an interview room first thing. His cold and soulless eyes stared straight ahead, refusing to shift attention from a spot on the wall behind Karen and Jade.

Karen had encountered many violent and dangerous criminals during her career, and Cready was up there with the best of them. DCI Scholes had mentioned that Cready's nickname was the Silent Assassin, and she understood why. Built like a brick shithouse with shoulders like boulders, he cast an intimidating presence, and one that must have terrified his victims.

Tired and hungry, Karen and Jade still needed to push on as they were against the clock. Jade did the introductions for the benefit of the recorder.

Karen shuffled through her notes before looking up at Cready, who refused to make eye contact with her. "What is the reason you entered the property last night?"

Silence.

"You torture and brutalise your victims in a unique way. And we believe you were responsible for murdering William Armstrong. We have a witness that can place you at the scene in his final few hours. Did you kill him?"

Silence.

"We also believe you were responsible for the murder of his brother, Michael Armstrong. You attacked, tortured and murdered him in your effort to track down his brother. Did you murder him?"

Silence.

It was going to be another one of those one-sided interviews that drove her to the boundaries of frustration. They had appointed Cready a duty solicitor, a woman in her mid to late forties, who sat beside him and made notes. She occasionally glanced at Karen and then to her client, hanging on Karen's every word before returning to her notes.

"We know from our colleagues in Manchester that you are a freelance enforcer for the criminal underworld. Who are you working for this time?" Karen pushed. She stared at him, looking for any sign of acknowledgement or reaction. Nothing. He was good. Very good.

"Do the names Lee or Paul Harman ring a bell?" she continued.

Silence.

"Okay, I'm going to take a wild stab in the dark and tell you what I'm thinking," Karen said flamboyantly waving her hand in the air. "I think Lee Harman employed you to find William Armstrong and recover the hundred and fifty thousand pounds William had embezzled from the business before he disappeared. Since William has been living outside of witness protection, Lee Harman has been trying his hardest to find William, and when he failed, he spoke to the Hasani firm. You know the Hasanis, don't you?" Karen said, furrowing her brow and pausing for a moment to look for any reaction in Cready's eyes. "Well, let's assume you do as you've done a fair bit of work for them. Lee Harman spoke to them, and they spoke to you, and well… You're here. Up shit creek."

Silence.

"You realise that the evidence is going to build up against you? We have sent your little goodie bag and clothes off for fast-track forensic analysis. The results will be back within the next twelve to twenty-four hours. You *could* make life a lot easier for yourself if you gave us the name of the person you're working for."

Silence.

Karen lifted the clear evidence bag containing his mobile phone. "An interesting sequence of messages on here. 'Your person found. Identity confirmed.' What does that mean? Who did you find?" Karen waited for an answer, but expected none, so continued. "And then a few hours later, 'Job done.' What job?"

Silence.

Karen gritted her teeth and eyed the man with contempt. "Okay, let's suspend the interview for the moment and return you back to your cell to have a good, long, hard think about your predicament, because as far as I can see, yesterday was your last day of freedom... ever."

Karen and Jade returned to the SCU. There was a good mood among the team and a sense of relief. Their high-risk operation during the night had resulted in the capture of their number-one suspect and now the hard work started to build a case against Dale Cready.

"How did it go?" Belinda asked as Jade and Karen grabbed a few empty chairs and sat down among the team.

Karen tutted. "I've got more chance of cracking a walnut between my thighs than breaking him. He's sticking to the criminal code. You don't grass. If he did, he wouldn't last a day in prison."

"He didn't utter a word in the interview. Not even a no comment or any kind of wind-up," Jade added. "He didn't even make *eye contact*."

"We wait for forensics?" Belinda asked.

"I think so," Karen said, picking up her mobile phone. "Start pulling all the files together for the CPS. The quicker we can get a charging sheet from them, the better."

---

KAREN STEPPED out of the building and did up the buttons on her jacket. The temperature had dropped a few degrees, and though not cold, the slight breeze whipped round her ankles. She took a couple of deep breaths to clear her head and flood her body with oxygen to reinvigorate her. She dialled Zac's number.

"Hey, you. We got him. The operation went as planned, and we got Dale Cready."

"That's fantastic news. Well done to you and the team. Was the super pleased?" Zac said.

"I've not told her yet. Jade and I have just come out of the interview and the team is now preparing the case file. I thought I'd call you first."

"Harman?"

Karen pulled a face. "I'm still working on that. Data from Cready's phone is being downloaded at the moment. We may be able to recover some deleted text messages. I know Lee Harman hired Cready. I need more evidence to prove that. The team is looking at Cready's financials. If we're lucky we might find a transaction between them."

"Harman wouldn't be careless enough to do it from an account with his name on it. Cready's payment would have come through a shell company, or another associate linked to Harman."

Karen knew Zac was right. Lee Harman was too slippery to make mistakes. But she remained hopeful. "Anyway, it's good news for you and Summer. Cready can't hurt either of you. Harman is in my crosshairs now. I'll see you this evening. I need to speak with the super."

"Okay, see you later. Love you," Zac replied.

## 51

WHILE THE TEAM waited the few weeks for forensics to come back to them, they continued working hard. As thanks, Karen rewarded her team members with a night out at a local Chinese restaurant. Team morale sometimes dipped after a tough case, and it was important in Karen's opinion to keep the team working well, but also give them the opportunity to let off steam. It hadn't been as easy to do back in London with so many officers commuting into the city from the neighbouring Home Counties. Her journey from Epping often took her at least an hour on a good day and two hours on a bad day when the tubes were playing up.

With most of her current officers living in and around York, it made it easier for them to enjoy some downtime together.

When Karen arrived the next morning, it appeared treating the team to an evening out had paid off. There was a lighter, relaxed atmosphere in the SCU. Officers were not only talking about the cases as they pulled together the various threads of the investigation, but they were talking about life, things going on at home, and early plans for Christmas.

"How are we getting on?" Karen asked as she wandered round the desks, sipping on her can of Red Bull.

"All good here," Ty replied. "We've downloaded the data from Cready's phone. There were hundreds of deleted messages we recovered and quite a few conversations linked to the Hasani firm. Definitely plenty of interesting threads which DCI Scholes should see."

"Great, I'll let him know to expect the data from you."

"There is also this," Ty added, handing Karen a sheet.

The sheet contained a list of dates and times along with GPS tracking data, and Karen's eyes kept shifting between the sheet and the whiteboard. "Yes! Just what we needed." The data points showed that Cready's phone was present at both Michael's and William's properties on the nights of their murder. The defence team would argue his phone may have been there, but it didn't confirm Cready's presence. They could argue Cready had lent his phone to another unknown individual, but thanks to Sharif, video evidence placed Cready at the scene on the night of William's murder, which was great news.

"Any news on forensics?" Karen asked no one in particular.

"Nothing yet," an officer shouted back from the rear of the room.

"Not to worry. I'll pop over now and see Bart. Call me if there are further developments," Karen shouted over her shoulder as she headed for the door.

She walked through the corridors, a lightness in her step from the relief she felt. Tying up loose ends always felt like it took ages. There were evidence logs to be checked and double-checked, exhibits to be documented correctly, and a timeline of events to be collated. They had plenty of time as it would be months before the case came to trial, but Karen was fastidious about detail, and it made sense in her eyes to do the legwork and preparation while the case was still fresh in everyone's minds.

Bart's team was in another building, and as she stepped out of her own, Karen came against a wall of drizzly rain. "Shit," she muttered, and not being fussed about grabbing a coat or umbrella, she hurried along between the buildings before diving into the one housing forensics services.

"Is Bart not round?" Karen asked, standing by the open door to his office.

An assistant close by confirmed he was tied up in a meeting.

Karen glanced round the floor until she spotted a CSI that she had worked with before and made a beeline for his desk. "Hi, Callum. I know Bart is in a meeting, but I wondered if my fast-track request was back?"

Callum smiled and prodded his glasses to the bridge of his nose. He was a quiet individual known for his thoroughness and attention to detail. "Let me check," he said, turning to his computer. It took a few moments as he scanned through his inbox. "Yes, the results came through about thirty minutes ago. I'm sure Bart would have called you the moment he was out of his meeting."

"Yeah, I know. Can you give me the headlines?"

"Sure." Callum scanned the details looking for the results. "Okay, they identified DNA traces trapped between the blades on the tin snip. Further analysis confirmed a DNA match for William Armstrong... and... Michael Armstrong."

Karen's eyes widened in surprise.

"There was also a DNA and print match on the handles belonging to Dale Cready. Oh, they also found another microscopic blood smear caught in a scuff mark on the handle and extracted a DNA sample from it. There's no match on the system, but there's a partial match with a victim of a serious assault. Ciaran Ackley." Callum turned towards Karen. "Does any of that help?"

Karen smiled. "It more than helps. Is that all of it?"

"Let me check." Callum scanned through the various pages of the report. "There's a fair bit more for you to work through, but they found a small, bloodied hair fibre trapped in the grip on the sole of Dale's right black Nike trainer. Hair fibre analysis confirms a match with William Armstrong."

Karen's skin prickled with excitement. Forensics had come through with an avalanche of evidence confirming Dale Cready as the murderer of the Armstrong brothers and Ackley's assailant. In Karen's opinion, it couldn't get any better. She thanked Callum before hurrying back to her team to break the news. They could charge Cready with two murders and GBH on Ackley. Now it was time to bring in the big fish.

## 52

"You can't go up there!" the ground-floor receptionist yelled as Karen and her team stormed through the lobby towards the elevators.

"I can," Karen shouted back, "and if you try to stop me, they'll arrest you for obstruction. Frankly, I doubt you're paid enough for that grief." Karen punched the button and waited, all the while watching the receptionist flapping in panic behind the desk, as she reached for her phone and stabbed wildly at the buttons. Karen couldn't help but smirk as she watched the scene unfold before her.

Karen instructed two officers to stay in reception to stop anyone from leaving the building.

After a few moments, the elevator bell chimed and the doors opened. Karen and half a dozen officers piled in and took the brief journey up before spilling out into the first-floor reception. The news of their arrival had caused a stir as three heavies marched along the corridor in Karen's direction. They stopped feet away from Karen and blocked access.

"I'm sorry. This is private property, and you have no right to go any further," one heavy growled as he puffed out his muscly chest and pushed his shoulders back to widen his appearance.

"You're right, and I probably need a warrant. I'm not sure if I've got one?" Karen said with a wry smile, patting down the front of her jacket and then the pockets on her trousers.

"I think this is what you're looking for," Ty said, stepping forward to hand Karen the warrant.

Karen smiled. "Oh, look. I've got an arrest warrant for Lee Harman. Now I suggest you move to one side and let us do our work. If you obstruct us or lay a finger on us, I'll arrest you so quickly and have you thrown in a van, you won't get time to fart. Now get out of my bloody way," Karen said, staring down the heavy closest to her.

The heavies glanced at each other nervously before moving to one side as Karen and the team rushed by. As they turned the corner, two further heavies blocked the door to Lee Harman's office.

Karen waved the arrest warrant as she approached. "Get out of my way, or you'll be arrested for obstruction like your other meathead mates back there," Karen said, nodding back in the direction from which they had come.

Dan was the only member of Karen's team who was the same muscly shape and size as these two burly minders, so he stepped round Karen and manhandled the men out of the way, their weak objections falling on deaf ears. Karen opened the door to see Lee Harman sat at his desk, his mouth open, a look of surprise on his face.

"Have you come back for more?" he asked.

Karen approached his desk and slapped the warrant down. Harman glanced down at the paperwork as his heavies piled through the door behind Karen's team and took up positions round the room, hoping the show of force would intimidate their uninvited guests.

"I thought I'd let you know that we have Dale Cready in custody. We have charged him with the murders of Michael and William Armstrong," Karen said.

Lee Harman remained composed, not an ounce of concern etched on his features. "And? I've never heard of the man before?"

"Oh, I think you have." Karen retrieved a clear evidence bag from inside her jacket containing a mobile phone. "This is Cready's phone, and we found a series of text messages to an unknown number. We believe they were in relation to not only identifying Michael and William Armstrong, but also confirming they had been killed. Whoever this number belongs to is the person who employed Cready to do his dirty work for him."

Harman glared at the phone for a few seconds before looking back at Karen.

Karen dialled the number and waited for it to connect as she glanced round the room at the heavies, wondering which phone would ring. A phone rang in Harman's direction. Karen spun round to see the look of shock on Harman's face as a phone vibrated inside his jacket pocket.

"Go on, answer it."

Harman's eyes flickered as he reached inside his jacket pocket and pulled out a phone.

Karen nodded at him to continue.

Harman placed the phone to his ear and answered.

"Gotcha," Karen said down the line. "I'm arresting you for being complicit in the murders of William and Michael Armstrong. We also discovered a payment made a week before Michael Armstrong was murdered for the sum of twenty thousand pounds. The account is in the name of Daryl Roberts. We found a passport in that name in Cready's possession. The passport photo matches Cready. We traced the payment you made back to a subsidiary company of yours. You are also being arrested for fraud, bribery, and witness intimidation."

Dan and Ty came round to Harman's side of the desk and hauled him up from his chair before cuffing his hands behind him. Further officers moved in to handcuff Harman's heavies.

Karen stepped in and stood inches away from Harman, keeping eye contact even though she caught a whiff of his stale breath. "I'll make sure you go away for a very long time. You're over. I'll make sure we expose every connection and contact you have. Take him downstairs." Karen stepped back as Dan and Ty jostled Harman forward.

"You're nothing. You think it's over?" Harman spat. "You haven't got a clue who you're messing with. Your day will come."

Karen folded her arms across her chest and smiled as they hauled Harman across his office to the door. "I'll be waiting."

Harman paused in the doorway and gritted his teeth before laughing. "Trust me, you have bigger problems coming your way. Sally Connell slipped back into the country six weeks ago."

Karen's heart pounded, and her breath caught. She froze, her stomach twisting into knots, the name Sally Connell echoing like a sinister omen.

## CURRENT BOOK LIST

Hop over to my website for a current list of books:

http://jaynadal.com/current-books/

## ABOUT THE AUTHOR

Author of:

The DI Scott Baker Crime Series

The DI Karen Heath Crime Series

The Thomas Cade PI Series

Printed in Great Britain
by Amazon